Home in Exile

Home in Exile

Felix Kobla Wornameh

authorHOUSE®

AuthorHouse™
1663 Liberty Drive
Bloomington, IN 47403
www.authorhouse.com
Phone: 1-800-839-8640

Published by AuthorHouse   09/11/2012

ISBN: 978-1-4678-7752-7 (sc)
ISBN: 978-1-4678-7753-4 (e)

Dedication

This novel is dedicated to all migrants and, the people of Ketu North District, Volta region Ghana

Biography

Credits to the loving Japanese wife Megumi Wornameh who motivated the husband to get back to school in his late thirties to develop his passion, Felix said, he would never have found the excitement for writing.

He moved from Japan and enrolled at the University of East London Law school England in 2009, due to graduate in June 2012. He also attended WASS and ATTRACO, all in Ghana.

Felix Kobla Wornameh whose hometown is Dzodze—Ketu North, grew up in a poor but, modest family in Ghana. His childhood and adult life had been nothing more than survival. His favorite sense in that situation was the first day he was sent to school to learn English language in a make-shift structure in Nima, the largest slum in Ghana.

This realization is part of the reason for so much sympathy for immigrants, He became fascinated on knowing how hard and unprecedented some families have tried to make it in life.

Geographical Locations

Some sand dunes reached 590 ft in height. The name Sahara comes from the Arabic word meaning; The Great Desert.

Apart from the Antarctica, it is the world's largest desert spread over 9,400,000 square kilometers

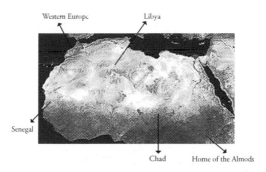

The Sahara covers most of Northern Africa making it almost as large as Europe or the United States size. It stretches from the Red Sea, including parts of the Mediterranean coasts, almost to the outskirts of the Atlantic Ocean.

To the south, it is bounded by the Sahel, a belt of semi-arid tropical savanna that runs across six countries from Senegal to Chad

Acknowledgement

"I'm heartily thankful to the entire students and staff of UEL. The law school in particular, Fiona Fairweather, Sharon Levy, Alan Wilson, Dr Hilary Lim, Elizabeth Stokes and Lawrencin George whose encouragement, guidance and support from the initial stages to the final level of my studies enabled me develop.

I offer my regards and blessings to all those who through thick and thin supported me with words of encouragement in all respect during the completion of this project. I can not help but mention Alfred Amamoo, Mr and Mrs. Stephen Sey, Bright Kolani, Dorah Chucumba, Ugo Samuel and Hannah Olorunu. Least I forget all the lovely Reach co workers at Heathrow Airport.

The last but not the least, I owe my deepest gratitude to my wife Megumi Wornameh and to all the Wornameh family for their staunch moral support throughout the project span, and significantly Efo W.K Selase who made available his pertinent support in diverse ways culminating to the introduction of this book"

Inroduction

The book, 'HOME IN EXILE' attempts to give a vivid account of the perils migrants go through in their determination to reach Europe in search of greener pasture.

The publication of this novel is most timely and is highly recommended to all and sundry specially the youth who in their exuberance are contemplating on embarking on a trekking trip across the desert en-route to Europe via Libya, Algeria, and Morocco over the Mediterranean Sea, to ponder seriously it over to enable them realize the precarious journey that waits them.

The novel captures the callous *World* of African migrants saddled with extortion, rape, torture, murder, drugs and arms couriering. Not only had despotic democratic tendencies of governments in the sub-region been brought to the glare, but the general sense of disillusionment among the teeming youth. This is what precipitates the arduous journey through the vast and rugged desert, Sahara.

Many had perished on these journeys and continue to but few, very few were lucky to have scaled through and the author is. Only the valiant dares. Felix Kobla Wornameh has in his literary piece has bequeathed posterity a timely warning, 'beware of crossing the Sahara'

Efo W.K.Selase, January 2012 Accra,Ghana.

One

The starless cloudy night was darker than usual. Faint footsteps sounded in the distance then subsequently stopped. The girls heard it again. This time the slow-paced footsteps grew louder and louder, coming towards the main entrance of the house. They died out at the door. A few seconds passed in silence.

'Put out the lantern,' whispered one of the girls. Alima gestured towards Benatu, who tiptoed nervously towards the lantern and snuffed it. All four girls held their breath and clung to each other, silently reciting multilingual incantations. The old clock ticked in the background of the tense atmosphere.

Suddenly, there was a gentle twist of the door handle; the girls turned towards the door trembling all over. But it soon stopped. There was a brief attempt again on the handle and then, unexpectedly, the footsteps retreated. The girls did not move but carefully listened until the footsteps had died away in the distance.

That the owner of those footsteps would return soon to break down the door was very certain; knowing this sent a shiver down the girls' spines. Alima bit her lips, took a deep breath, and gestured for her sisters to get onto their feet.

Alima's courage and logical thinking was an exact replica of that of her father, who lay on the floor dead. She struggled to face the reality that she and her sisters had become orphaned children within an hour of coming home and that she was faced with the task of smuggling out and raising her three younger sisters without any generosity from her immediate environment.

It had been a long-standing tradition in the war-ravaged country of Kumalis, controlled by the Anchike Islamic militants, that families were torn apart with brute force.

Fighting and violent deaths were a daily occurrence.

Women who resisted being given away for marriage could be accused falsely of adultery, and the repercussion was often very ugly. This was a place where a rapist often went free, whilst victims who found themselves raped were often accused of adultery.

The airwaves frequently buzzed with headlines, such as, 'Child Suffers Horrendous Death at the Behest of Armed Opposition Groups'. And the most recent told of a thirteen-year-old-girl who was stoned to death after being accused and found guilty of adultery by a militant court.

The Almonds were no exception. The four girls hailed from the village of Bassata in northern Kumalis in the southern part of East Africa.

Alima, age fifteen, was the eldest; she was well built, with a rather typical boyish looks and charisma. Talima, age thirteen, was the second born. Next was Benatu, age twelve, followed by the youngest, Koshi, age eleven.

The four girls had been born to Mr Alidu Almond and Madam Wamunatu Koshi, who died during the birth of Koshi. As a result of the serious complications leading to her mother's death, Koshi had become deaf and mute.

Together with their father, the girls had resisted being given away in a forced marriage to Alhaaj Dornucho, leader of the Anchike rebel tribesmen. As a consequence, the girls, upon arrival home one evening after school, had found their father shot in the stomach.

As the daughters circled around their dying father, he spoke in a diminishing voice. 'They will come back for you girls,' he said. 'Just go.' Blood oozed from his mouth as he struggled to continue. 'Go,' he urged, 'far, far away from them.'

He closed his eyes briefly and opened them again to look at the girls. He raised his eyes towards the heavens and said something in a faint whisper.

Alima leaned forward on her knees and, with one hand cupped behind her left ear, asked gently, 'Sorry, Dad, what did you say?'

With an enormous effort, he had managed in a faint audible voice to say, 'I will see you all in heaven.'

In fear for their lives, Alima now rallied her other sisters and stormed their late dad's closet. She got a scissors and shortened each of her sister's hair into boyish-looking styles.

The girls quickly got rid of their earrings.

Alima drilled her sisters on how to walk without anyone detecting that they were females. 'Do not talk,' she said.

'Guys are more relaxed than girls; this keeps them from being open for questioning, just take it easy and look at no one twice.'

They all shaved their leg hair, wore no make-up, made their faces slightly dirty, donned baggy trousers from the lot, and fastened tight ace bandages around their tops to reduce their chest size. When each added an oversized sweater and a baseball cap to the ensembles, they had perfectly boyish looks.

But before they set out, Koshi made an important gesture.

She signalled to the rest of the sisters that some people could determine a person's gender by looking at his or her throat. Some boys had Adam's apples, whilst girls, in most cases, didn't. So, the sisters decided to wear turtleneck sweaters instead. Unable to find a turtleneck of the right size, Koshi, wore a scarf around her throat. It was February

1991, late winter, so the weather was conducive to their warm dress.

Disguised in male clothing, the girls quickly changed names. Alima easily turned into the masculine *Ali*. Talima became *Taba*, and Benatu shortened to *Ben*.

The youngest sister had been named after the girls' late mother, whose first name was Koshi. Koshi remained the name of the youngest, since it's a Theophanous name for both sexes

In five minutes, they got acquainted with their new names and advanced towards the door, hoping to sneak out under cover of darkness. They had only one purpose in mind—getting to England, where you could be free.

'But I am—' *Taba* choked. 'I'm—scared.' Her voice sounded dejected. 'I mean, how—? How can we make it?

"you remember Dad once told us how equally dangerous our bordering counties are?"

"We are faced with the task of crossing over hundreds of miles of—'

'Stop! Stop it,' retorted *Ali* bodily, moving towards her sister. 'Look at me,' she said, struggling to hold her tears back and hugging *Taba*. 'I know it's not going to be easy, but we have no choice. The only other option is to stay here and die a miserable death. We must take this risk so that we might find freedom.'

'I know, but how?' *Taba* insisted. 'We are not only battling against the miles, but we must also sneaking through four Sharia law-infested countries, where all women are forbidden to walk alone in public, much less the young unmarried women,' she lamented.

A brief silence fell among the sisters. Finally, they moved towards the front door. *Ali n*ervously bit her lips; the younger sisters nervously rubbed their hands over their faces as they unlocked the front door.

They scanned the dark compound carefully. Nothing made noise except the breezy wind that swayed the branches of the big baobab tree that stood right in the middle of the compound.

A nagging doubt that someone was hiding nearby ready to pounce on them made the sisters wait with tensed and bated breath for a few seconds. The consequences if they were caught trying to escape would be very hostile.

Conceivably, we could just give up, report to the tribal leaders, and be taken as slave brides, and perhaps if we could show some dedication and be submissive to every demand of the rebels, we might be treated well, Ali thought.

Although she was aware that being caught trying to escape would erase the small chance that their lives would be spared, the thought of her younger sisters being raped by the rebels was far more depressing for her than losing her life.

This thought gave her the final push, and she stepped out of the door quickly and flattened herself against the wall, using the baobab tree's shadow as her cover. She could hear her own heart beating.

She froze for a while, and then she craned her head backwards to look behind the tree. Her heartbeat raced as she observed two male figures standing and talking to each other in a low, hushed tone.

Without further comment, she flattened herself on the ground and signalled her sisters to do the same. They held their breaths and started crawling on their bellies towards a heap of rubbish 15 metres away on the left adjacent to their structure.

The eldest three quickly arrived at their destination and looked on anxiously as the youngest gave up and spread out her hands in exhaustion after 10 metres. Hearing the footsteps approach the main door on the far side, *Ali* could not wait any longer. She rushed and grabbed her little sister from the ground, and the four girls made their way into the night.

*   *   *

A mile soon became two; then tens turned into hundreds.

Within two weeks, the sisters were cramped in a Toyota Land Cruiser with other migrants, heading towards Northern Algeria.

The driver pressed on, covering quite a distance. Before the day's heat soared to about a hundred degrees, the Almonds were having lunch in an unknown part of the Saharan desert with the only shelter formed by the vehicle's shadow.

After another marathon drive, they started advancing through scattered rocky hills and strange valleys.

As the darkness advanced, the horrible heat of the Sahara started to diminish and became friendly. They came to a halt as visibility became more difficult, and the spot where they stopped turned out to be their temporary shelter for the night. Each of the sisters had a meal and stretched her limbs, ready to fall into the deep sleep of the fatigued.

Barely awake, they heard at a far distance a roar of an engine and saw a searching beam of light. Not aware of what or who it might be, their driver judged it prudent to put themselves in a state of cover. He ordered all of his passengers to lay flat on their backs. All obeyed, lying with hands pressed against their chest and bated breath.

Unexpectedly, the passengers heard a cry from the driver and his mate. 'Kai! Kai! Haya! Haya!' they called, ordering all to get on board as quickly as possible.

Within a twinkle of an eye, the passengers had all been seated, and the driver drove off, driving erratically deep into the night. They drove without headlights until the vehicle was swallowed up in a strange part of the desert.

When the Land Cruiser had finally come to a stop, the girls learned that they had fled in order to avoid arrest. The driver had deemed the beam of light they had seen to belong to anti-smuggling patrol guards. They passed the remainder of the night there.

The group was distressed when daylight advanced and, before embarking again upon the journey, a head count detected one person missing. No frantic effort by the driver to retrace their steps or relocate the spot from where they had fled was possible.

Over the remainder of their journey towards Djanet, the Almonds thought of the missing man often, wondering what might have befallen this innocent soul lost in the desert. Had he slept through the shouts alerting the group of their attempt to outwit the patrol guards? Or had he fallen out of the vehicle as it had sped erratically through the night? They kept on asking each other these questions, to which no answers would ever come.

Two

In between two large rocks, the Toyota Land Cruiser screeched to a final halt. Signalling that his vehicle had accomplished its journey, the driver rolled down his side window and stretched out his left arm, pointing with his index finger in the direction of the Djanet Township.

All the migrants were ordered down and, in very little time, had sped off. But before they went, the driver cautioned them to take extra precautions during this portion of the trip, as they crept into the town. The police in this part of the Saharan city preyed on illegal immigrants.

A group of twelve, the travellers judged it wise to reduce their number and divided themselves into two groups of six, each group taking a different route into town.

One group adopted the normal way of ascending a rock until they caught a glimpse of the town. It worked to perfection. But the trouble was deciding how to sneak in unnoticed.

The other group thought it wise to have a rest in a grotto nearby and to approach the town at dusk, thus giving them the chance to stretch their limbs. Some of the group dozed off for a bit.

This second group, which included the disguised Almonds, approached the town as darkness advanced in absolute silence. On seeing a friendly young man in a farmhouse, they settled in.

In no time, the young man hastened to ask about their mission.

'We are on a journey to Europe via Libya,' Bala, the group leader, hastily disclosed.

'Ah!' the young man exclaimed, 'I am a master tactician when it comes to the journey from here to Garth. I am the best escort within miles of this place,' he concluded.

These words were sonorous to the travellers' ears, and the group was extremely pleased.

'But, which vehicle will you send us with?' asked Bala.

'Oh—er—no!' the guide cried. 'You don't go by car from here into Libya, unless you have a visa or permit or—. Do you hold one?' he asked.

'How do we get there then?' enquired Bala.

'Er—the journey from here is a four-day trek through the Ahaggar Terrain,' he explained.

Thus, the guide had opened the lid containing the unspoken rumour, which none of the migrants had ever believed.

They shook their heads in disbelief.

The young man also shook his head, and then he went on.

'We shall spend a night at the foot of the mountain and climb the next dawn, before embarking on the main trek.'

There was no option. Each member of the group obliged, vowing to risk the journey. The young man guided them to the village centre to get additional food, biscuits, and other necessities in preparation for the journey the following night.

*   *   *

For unknown reasons, the guide postponed the trip to the next night. This was a big blow to some of the immigrants due to their strict budgets; another day spent waiting meant they had to spend extra on food and lodging.

They hastily assembled for the trip the second night.

Eagerness and unspoken fear hovered within each member of the group, for they were beginning a trip that would either better their lives or destroy them.

The guide had asked the group to call him Billy. Many wondered why he fancied such name.

Billy broke the morning silence by saying, 'I have another group waiting in a nearby farm village, so we shall move quietly and make a stopover. And together, we shall make the trip.'

None of the migrants complained or even spoke a word.

'Can I collect my fee first?' the guide requested.

'Yes,' replied Bala.

Billy collected forty dinars from each of the migrants, placing the money in his hat to keep it safe. 'Okay, let's go,' he said.

The group moved into the night, which was even darker than any of the migrants were accustomed to. Thirty minutes later they had joined the other group, a much larger one, bringing their number to thirty-seven.

As they continued their exodus, no one uttered a word. The atmosphere seemed relaxed but intimidating. The pace soon quickened, and some were virtually jogging to catch up.

The group followed the young man for about four hours without a moment's rest, for he was racing to beat the daylight and to avoid being exposed to the community.

Nothing penetrated the dreadful silence, except the crackling of individual boots on the occasional stone.

Finally, they came to a sudden stop at the foot of a huge dark image. All wondered what loomed before them.

Whispering, the guide broke the silence. 'These are the Ahaggar Mountains; we shall spend the remaining night here and climb it at dawn.'

Earlier in the day, Billy had pointed to what seemed to be more of a hill than a mountain, saying it was the mountain they would be ascending. From a distance, it had seemed both low and near, and the travellers were all shocked at the sheer massiveness of their impending ascent. 'Oh,' little *Koshi* groaned, wincing at the gruelling distance they had covered to reach the mountain and, worse, tomorrow's journey. The image of the mountain in the dark was a horrific sight.

Together, the group passed the night in the open dark, cold, and miserable desert.

Soon, Billy called for everyone to get prepared for the climb, as daylight had started to take over from the night.

After a critical observation, he asked the group to follow his trail as he carefully ascended the part of the mountain that had the gentlest slope and wider cracks they could hold onto to catch their breaths. The climb was even more than they had anticipated. It took hours to get to the peak.

But their greatest displeasure was the sight of another giant looming mountain.

The disguised sisters remained anonymous and silent throughout the climb. However, Bala, together with another immigrant, decided to question the escort, verifying what he had told them earlier—that after ascending the second mountain, they could see the outskirts of their next destination.

Billy answered with a warm smile, 'Oh, don't worry! As soon as we overcome the next peak, you will see the countryside of your next destination even clearer.'

At the conclusion of these words, he took leave of them.

The words were so perfect that the travellers were delighted and no one gave the guide's assurances a second thought.

Hastily, they descended and forced themselves to begin ascending the next mountain, only to see the chain of Algerian mountains shimmering like a mirage far into the horizon. By then, the morning heat had soared to over 100 degrees Celsius. They heard no sound of living things; everything they could see looked barren.

'We have been deceived.' said one aspiring migrant calmly.

All of the travellers turn towards him, acknowledging the truth of what he'd said by nodding their heads.

'And worst of all, we have also nearly emptied our gallons of water,' *Ali* added in a whisper.

Bala turned around to take a second look at the jagged edge and then stiffened. 'Ah,' he whispered, sucking in his breath and taking a nervous step forward to ascertain what he had just seen. Joining him, the others, gripped by unspoken fear, let their jaws drop open.

At least three scorched preserved bodies lay within a 2-meter radius of rocky ground in this part of the Ahaggar Plateau.

Disembodied limbs, clothing, and belongings were strewn about haphazardly; what looked like a chopped skull rolled to a halt a few meters away from the carnage.s

The dead looked shrunk and pitch black in the heat. They did not smell. They did not buzz with flies. They had been butchered a couple of days earlier and had been highly preserved by the dry, hot Saharan desert. Thus, the crime scene remained exactly the same, uncontaminated.

Away from the bodies lay scattered clothing, an axe stained with dried blood, and a cutlass. Skin hung from the deserted blades. Dismembered feet and an arm lay a short distant away from the body of a little girl. Bruises covered her face and torso. Her legs were spread out, and her big toe was torn apart.

This was a few years after the peak of the Tuareg uprising in the early 1990s. Tuareg peoples formed a distinct minority in all the Saharan countries. They dwelled in many Saharan regions. In many cases, poverty, as a result of desertification and age-long droughts, forced the Tuareg's to change their traditional migration routes.

In addition, the harsh desert conditions, compounded with lack of aid from the national government, resulted in increased conflict between neighbouring Tuareg groups.

Fuelled by that, large number of Tuareg nomads fled, whilst others made their way to refugee camps in neighbouring countries; some roamed the vast desert for survival. A few who blamed their respective national governments for failing to aid communities in need commingled and formed rebel groups. And it was believed that some of these small Tuareg rebels groups had been carrying out atrocities on poor migrants found wanting in the harsh Ahaggars Terrains.

Most of the migrants had heard such rumours before, and the stories, coupled with the horrific scene, set the entire thirty-seven, mostly sub-Saharan immigrants on a quest to reaching the shores of Europe trembling. Among this group of immigrants were two Kenyans and the Almonds. The predominant were the West Africans from Ghana, Nigeria, Senegal, Cameroon and Mali.

Three

'We have to leave this place as soon as possible,' cried Bala.

Halfway into the retreat down the other side of the mountain, seven of the group, with no water and short of breath, felt too tired to continue and decided to give up for a moment and get some rest.

Their excessive exertions had taken a toll, but weariness has blurred their fears. Then unexpectedly, they encountered another set up corpses. This time, a woman and what seemed like a child were coiled together in a cloth wrap, lying five metres away from where the exhausted group wanted to rest. Both corpses lay sideways facing each, a hollow space between their torsos. The woman's left leg and both arms were slightly spread on a decaying cloth over the child's corpse. Her head was slightly tipped back, and her mouth was open.

Taba, Ali, and *Ben*, aided their little sister *Koshi* and continued.

They yelled at the remaining members of the group to follow up. But the seven remained were they were, curled over dejectedly, their faces in between their legs as a way of seeking some shelter from the horror and the desert sun.

By the time the Almond family descended the second mountain, they were panting excessively with mouths widely open. Too weak and badly damaged by dehydration to do anything else, they lay flat on their stomachs with their faces down. Soon, they were overtaken by the darkness, marking day one.

*   *   *

Having slightly regained their energy in the absence of the sun, the migrants decided to walk on. The valleys led into one another; they found themselves desperately walking from one end to another until the next morning dawned and were, apparently, soon finished off by the pitiless rising desert sun.

*   *   *

The Almonds now gave up their rucksack bags with the bag's content; the weight of the bags greatly hindered their weak and feeble limbs. *Ali,* on her part, took out two tins of sardines and handed over her remaining food to the earth.

By this time, the intensity of the desert heat had reached its peak, forcing all to retire. *Ali* managed to stagger away from the group. But she woefully failed to reach any human settlement by the time the next darkness took over.

She made a little effort to walk in the dark, but she only stumbled and fell over. Unable to move, she decided to spend the night where she lay.

Even though the heat of the day had been oppressing, she found herself inconvenienced by the desert's coldness at night. She endeavoured to keep awake out of fear of being attacked by a predator.

At the dawn of the third day, *Ali* had no idea where her family or the rest of the group were.

Despite being rendered very weak, she decided to try with all her might to reach the top of another mountain, with the hope of catching a glimpse of a nearby town. At the thought of that, she quickly disposed off her torn sneakers, her pant, and her jacket to loosen the weight on her feeble legs, but she managed to keep a tin of sardines in her hand.

Despite having shed all of that weight, she could hardly walk. Each step she took seemed to last centuries. Bit by bit, she managed to pull herself on her bottom towards the top of the mountain, her hopes high. Finally, she reached the top. She could see nothing but a chain of rocks stretching to the horizon. Out of shock and loss of hope, she started to shiver. *No*, she thought bitterly. She glanced slowly downwards and thought, *How can I descend?*

Unable to comfort herself, she felt tears form in her eyes, and soon she was crying uncontrollably.

She sought a spot her last resting place, feeling inclined towards a detached stone halfway down the slope she was on. Unable to control her thirst for water, she opened the sardine tin and used the top to trap her urine so she could drink it. She raised the container slowly towards her mouth. The stench was overwhelming, and she gave up.

She remained where she was, expecting to die before the next day. This was day four in the wilderness with no food, no water, and no escape from the heat.

* * *

The desert heat soon soared to its peak. *Ali* was still alive but badly in need of some liquid to keep her heart from dying of thirst. She managed to strip and carefully released urine into the sardine tin for the second time. This time, the magnitude of her thirst superseded any description on earth. She greedily drunk the urine and was still not comforted. She drank her urine over and over again until it ceased to flow because she was so dehydrated.

She remained in her spot, thinking of nothing except death.

I wish I could die now, she thought wearily.

Surprisingly, *Ali* survived the heat of the day, and when daylight advanced into night, she remained alive. She was resting on her back, motionless, when the desert silence was broken by a groaning sound.

Her only possible reaction on hearing the sounds of what she presumed to be an approaching predator was to stretch her scrawny neck and turn slowly in the direction the noise was coming from.

At that instant, she decided that it would be wise to get herself into a position of defence. But she was too weak and fragile to move, let alone stand on two feet. Quietly, she remained in the same position. She wasn't really afraid of being killed, but she was concerned about the extra pain she would undergo from the attack.

When the 'predator' moved into her line of sight, she sighed wearily. It was a wild camel. Thinking it might be accompanied by a human being, *Ali* made faint shouts to draw attention to herself. Nothing real came out of it.

Midway into the night, she fell asleep.

Day five arrived soon. *Ali* had now waited death for what seemed a very long time. The thought of jumping from her resting place to end her life became increasingly appealing.

Slowly, she gazed downwards. She tried to rise to her feet.

Each time she took a breath of air, her lungs seemed to explode. The thought of wounds and pains, coupled with her inability to stand on two feet, made her suicidal thoughts fade away.

Finally, she squeezed herself into a small grotto with the intention of dying there. Hallucinations soon took control.

She engaged herself in a brief conversation that was peppered with laughter. She stretched her arms open, as if she were hugging someone. Finally, she blacked out.

Four

Awakened all of a sudden by the raging of the wind, *Ali* observed with shock the change in the clouds. It seemed as if a rainstorm was coming.

But how can this be? she wondered, confused. She knew very well that this mountainous desert region normally received no rain throughout the year. The Sahara Desert lay in the middle of the equator. Air masses around this region tended to be too dry for precipitation.

But soon, hope throbbed in her clumped bosom as she beheld the first drops of rain and felt the wetness tingle her body. With nothing to trap the water, she opened her mouth as wide as she could. The drops seemed far from what she needed. After a few minutes, she was drenched and felt slightly refreshed.

She managed to gaze down beneath where she was lying and caught sight of a bowl-sized crater filled to the brim with water. 'Ha,' she murmured.

She descended on her bottom with renewed vigour at the sight of the water. She bent and took sip after sip without any thought as to how unclean the water might be.

A few minute passed, and she struggled to get up. She fell and tried again. This time, she rose successfully but with great difficulty. Before long, she adhered to nature's call—needing to use the toilet for the first time in nearly five days.

She staggered along with short breaks and occasional falls and, in the process, found some strange animals horns. She didn't worry much about which animal the horns might have belonged to. She grabbed two out of the horns and filled them with the dirty brownish-looking water and sipped from her makeshift cup until her stomach was full.

Then she proceeded on her journey.

Gradually, she descended, staggering aimlessly, her feet bare, deep into the valley. Unaware of the multiple cuts and bruises she sustained, she just kept staggering on.

After some time, she paused and took a glance at the jagged valley that stretched out in front of her. She spotted a whitish moving figure. Wiping her eyes in disbelief, she saw the same figure, only this time more clearly—a man dressed in an all-white Arabian gown with his turban veil firmly tied over his head.

Ali approach the first human she had seen in nearly five days as fast as her feeble legs could carry her.

She cried out in a voice full of cracks, grief, and longing when she got closer to the figure.

When the man caught sight of Ali, he was, at first, gripped with fear. He looked at *Ali* as if an evil fairy had crossed his path.

Then he seemed to relax and watched with no further surprise as the pale skinny lost migrant approached him. *Ali* didn't take her eyes off him and moved towards him with little concern that she would be exposed as a female. This man, whom *Ali* knew later to be called Abass, knew exactly what might have happened to her.

With the tradition of mostly male immigrants found wanting in the desert, Abass had not a single doubt as to the disguised, frail-looking *Ali's* gender. To her great relief, he addressed her as a male. He took *Ali* by the hand so that she wouldn't fall and led her on. The man tried to ask her a question in an Arabic language. '*Shinu mushkila?*' (meaning?) But *Ali* couldn't understand.

They walked for about an hour and a half, taking an occasional rest for *Ali's* sake and, in the end, arrived at a military camp nearby, upon which the Good Samaritan,

Abass, took leave of her.

She was served French bread with camel meat soup. Her throat and tongue had swollen from dehydration. She couldn't eat the bread but managed some soup and fruit juice. The men in the camp offered her a shower. She accepted the offer and rested for two hours.

Later, Mr Abass returned with two young men who spoke some English to serve as interpreters. *Ali* soon told them about the fate of her brothers and the other immigrants.

A rescue crew was soon dispatched. Four hours later, they came back empty-handed. *Ali* shuttered; with no news whatsoever on any among the entire group of immigrants, including her sisters, she was devastated.

*   *   *

Two days later, *Ali* took a walk into the Djanet Township.

She hoped to find means to return to her home country.

She learnt with horror that two bodies had been discovered in the mountains and was also told that making the long journey back home would be more treacherous than going forward.

Unable to ascertain any details about her family and the other travellers, she chose to join a new group of immigrants in town to make the three-day walk to Libya. This time,

Ali met nine illegal immigrants—three young men from Nigeria and five other young men from Niger Republic.

On the night before their departure, a local native brought three more immigrants, increasing their number to thirteen.

Ali was too sleepy to notice anyone in particular. They set off early in the morning in quite a similar fashion as the previous group had.

This time, they were with a genuine escort, Ali thought and hoped. They made it to the top of the Ahaggar Plateau in a procession, with *Ali* right behind their escort, before the crack of dawn. At the top of the Ahaggar, they encountered a totally different scenario. They beheld an extensive flat rocky surface stretching without end.

As visibility became clearer, the guide barked an order, '*Kai gams gams*,' signalling with a gesture that it was time for rest.

All of the migrants soon sat on the ground. Ali and the others used this opportunity to look at each other for the first time and acquaint themselves with their travelling companions.

She felt a sudden rush in her heartbeat when she caught sight of Koshi. She turned her gaze quickly back again, and to her surprise, saw her whole family among the group. The sisters rose quickly to their feet upon seeing each other.

'Ali!" murmured Ben, her mouth dropping open in disbelief.

Also in disbelief, Ali covered her mouth with both hands.

'Er—' She tried to talk, but she was speechless. She paused and waited in silence as the past and the present begun to merge again.

The other migrants watched as the two men clasped hands, without any suspicion about their gender. Ali learnt how Ben, Koshi, and Taba had been rescued by a native camel rider two days earlier. But she was sad to hear that a twin brother of one of the immigrants had died exactly at the place he'd collapsed. Luckily enough, his body had been retrieved and buried by the kind locals who rescued them.

The surviving twin had the opportunity to take and keep a bit of his brother's hair and nails, with the hope of sending these pieces of his brother to their home country for funeral rites, as custom demanded. He decided to withdraw from the forward journey.

For two days, the walk was fairly uneventful but rather exhausting. On the night of day two, the group beheld the outskirts of Libya, rejoicing at the sight of the dim lights far in the distance. With the greatest assurance of getting into Libya the next evening, they retired into a crater that was half the size of a soccer pitch, where they had their usual meal of hard biscuits, evaporated milk, and wild dates with fresh crater water. Everyone in the group slept soundly that night, partly because they had spent their day putting forth such great effort.

Daylight soon came. As they were on the final lap of their journey, each member of the group took some time to clean up and do away with unwanted baggage. All were in good spirits, and they engaged in a hearty conversation without fear for the first time in three days.

Then all of a sudden an explosion rang out. *Bam! Bam!* All conversations ceased abruptly; everyone was dead silent.

Emerging above them on the high rocks above the crater stood six men masked in black turban veils, wielding rifles and pistols with doubled-edged hatchets loosened in their sheaths.

Five

In the atmosphere of tranquility that had reigned moments earlier, it was difficult for the migrants to believe that they would have to face the callousness of the desert stories they had so often heard—that the fascinating and heartbreaking news could be real for them. Each day, a seemingly endless procession of men and women were on the move through this desert, with the hope of reaching Europe.

Back in Senegal, hundreds of sub-Saharan immigrants assembled along the shores with the slogan, 'See Europe or die!' They readied themselves to be cramped into aged wooden boats en route to Europe.

Meanwhile, over two hundred immigrants had just landed on the Tenerife coast packed in wooden boats. At the same time, in a small village in Malaysia, a group of young men were making their final preparation to migrate to Australia on board a cargo ship.

A man in Ajaguja who had just stabbed a taxi driver over a fare row was fleeing prosecution. He agitatedly joined other immigrants in Mauritania in search of any illegal route to Europe.

On this same day, there was news in Dover, United Kingdom, of the horrifying deaths of a group of men and women who were attempting to enter the country. The then secretary of state, Jack Straw, described their passing as the 'most terrible death' and issued a stark warning to other would-be illegal migrants. The airways and the Internet had been alive with reactions, some deploring the migrants and others sympathizing, following the death of fifty-eight Chinese immigrants who were sealed in a pitch-black lorry container and who had fought desperately amid soaring temperatures for air, clawing and banging at the locked steel door, to their deaths.

In Lakante, a village in the Central African Republic, a diviner was telling a young man, 'You are the light of your family and will be successful on your journey.' The diviner cautioned the young man, saying, 'To make this dream come true, you need to purify the gods with a white bull and a crate of dry Scottish whisky.'

So these armed men, aware that the procession of illegal migrants would always move through this terrain, were always on the lookout for prey. These six armed, masked men in turban veils soon became eight. Six descended into the crater, leaving two, wielding a 9 mm sub-machine gun and a rifle, on top of the crater.

The leader, in a green turban veil, gestured an order with both hands; the migrants' leader understood, obeyed, and signalled all to sit on the ground in two rows. Each immigrant was searched thoroughly and, if the masked men found no money, strip-searched and thoroughly beaten.

The Almonds whispered to each other and quickly made some cash available, ensuring it was easily seen, to avoid being strip-searched, hoping their true identities would, thus, go undetected.

The group's pockets and the lining of their bags and shoes were ripped open and searched. The gang kept a rather smiley look throughout their operation, to the relief of the frightened migrants.

Akim, one of the migrants who hailed from a rebel gang in Congo, was searched, but the men found nothing on him except a military identity card and a series of papers with some handwritten addresses. He was searched again, but nothing was found.

The gang leader, not convinced that Akim had no cash, shouted at him, 'Where is your money?!'

The relaxed approach of the armed men boosted Akim's level of arrogance. He replied, 'No money!' Then he intimated mildly, 'Fuck you.'

Unfortunately for Akim, the gang leader heard what he'd said and, without hesitation, two of the men jumped on Akim, slashing his waist. He yelled in horror, but they never stopped; they butchered him until he lay on the ground and made no further sound.

Every migrant cringed, clinging to each other. Most could not look on; nor could they believe what they had just seen.

'Surely, they will kill us all,' whispered Ali dejectedly to Taba.

While his men for dispatching of Akim, the gang's leader took a closer look at all the migrants. Koshi, the youngest of the Almonds, was eleven and a little chubby, though well disguised. But the gang leader in his green veil stiffened upon a second look at *Koshi*. His smile turned to a frown.

'*Kai, yala,*' he called to one of his assistants. And both, looking at *Koshi*, engaged in a discussion which none of the migrants understood. Although the Almonds didn't understand the men's language and dare to look at them, they knew both men had doubts about *Koshi* being a man and were contemplating.

For a few second, none of the men spoke. All paused and stiffened silently. Clutching *Ben's* hand tightly, the little girl shut her eyes and clenched her jaws so hard that it ached.

She glanced back slightly to see if the men had moved away from her. To her horror, the leader grabbed her, as she had feared. Now, looking at him, she made to move away. But she could not, for he had caught her firmly; she could feel his grip rigidly tighten.

Her face registered an expression of fear as the man stared at every inch of her face and waist. She was soon dragged forcefully away. When *Ali* and *Ben* took a step to intervene, a gun was raised at them. They froze, and the two robbers kept the guns on them without uttering a word. With every minute that passed, the possibility of them being shot or even detected as females increased. There was nothing the

Almonds could do other than to lower their gaze and step in line.

Koshi, though deaf and dumb, found the tone for frightened sobs. The shrillness of her cry and her intermittent vocalization was unbearable for the migrants, most of whom cried inwardly. A few blocks away, the poor girl glanced behind her, hoping to see her *family* in pursuant, to rescue her. But her horror increased as she saw no one coming after her. Soon, she had been pulled away from sight into a nearby cave.

A few seconds passed, and then a gunshot rang out.

Oh my God! Ali moaned inwardly, forcing her eyes shut so she would not shed tears.

Nothing was heard for about a minute, and then a clearing of a throat broke the silence. The leader emerged from the cave alone, to the worry of all.

He uttered a harsh word to his crew. Suddenly the remaining two armed men who had been waiting atop the crater descended into the crater with their hands on their guns.

Every indication pointed to the slaughter of the immigrants.

They felt it but were too terrified to move.

'*Kai, yala yala,*' said one of the men.

The leader groaned and uttered a word in return. Then he suddenly raced toward his mate. Both men paused and sniffed the air.

It seemed as if the cruelty of the migrants being shot was being hampered by internal unrest among the gang; none of the migrants could understand the robbers' arguments, but they knew something was amiss.

Whatever it was, to the disbelief of the migrants, dispelled the gloom; the robbers retreated quickly over the crater and disappeared in a manner similar to the way in which they'd come.

Six

After the gang had disappeared, the migrants remained where they sat, each still too terrified to move.

After about twenty seconds, *Ali* managed to regain her composure. She raced to the cave; the others regained consciousness and followed. '*Koshi*!' she called. '*Koshieee*!'

Ali shook her sister repeatedly and desperately, but there was no response. She paused and examined *Koshi's* body.

She found no trace of blood or a gunshot wound.

Then *Ben* shouted in joy, 'She is breathing!'

Taba heaved a sigh of relief. The sisters took a second look at *Koshi's* face.

She was beginning to regain consciousness, but they discovered that she had become very pale and distressed. Though deaf and, thus unable to speak, she could follow instructions and nod or shake her heard to answer 'yes' or 'no'.

She shook her head yes when asked if she had any pain and pointed to her abdomen. *Ali* and *Ben* ripped off her pair of trousers and found to their horror that, although she had not been raped as they feared, she was bleeding profusely from a stab in her lower abdomen.

As *Koshi* was unable to stand, *Taba* felt compelled to feel her sister's pulse. She first tried by going leaning in close, placing her left ear against *Koshi's* chest. The beat sounded irregular. Not satisfied, she reminded herself that the wrist was the easiest place to measure the pulse. She placed the tip of her index finger on *Koshi's* wrist below the base of her thumb, pressed lightly, and waited for a few seconds.

She could feel her sister's pulse distinctly, but the beat was not steady, and the rate was diminishing very quickly. The bleeding continued as well.

Ben, Ali, and *Taba* searched each other's faces, confused.

They were racing against an unknown task. And they had to act very quickly. All they knew was that they had to stem the blood flow if they had any chance of saving their poor sister.

'Er—' interrupted Soglo one of the migrants, a nurse in his native country, The Republic of Benin. Gently, he issued some first aid instructions. 'Let's position her to secure her airways,' he began.

'Airways?' asked Ali, who seemed not to understand what the nurse meant.

'I mean,' the young migrant continued, 'that the best thing to do is to elevate your sister's injury in order to use gravity to stem the blood flow.'

Sensing they still did not quite understand what he meant, the nurse moved in to help. He helped put *Koshi* in a reclining position, positioning her injured side up to allow blood to return to her heart. Two minutes passed, and she continued to bleed.

She soon blacked out.

'Let's go,' said *Taba* to the others.

They decided to carry *Koshi* for the remaining gruelling six-hour trek to the nearest human settlement, hoping that she might survive.

But barely an hour into the journey, she passed away.

The Almonds wept bitterly and were deeply saddened when they had to erect a stone monument over *Koshi's* body in the rocky desert and move on. *Ali*, being the eldest, cursed herself bitterly for not being able to protect her sister and reflected on their journey as meaningless.

Here we are, she thought, *over 3,000 miles away from our dream home, somewhere in the middle of the Saharan desert, and the dream of a free life in England has ended for little Koshi.*

The rest of the group, though grieved and devastated, had to move on.

The remaining six hours of the journey was uneventful, but every step was overshadowed by fresh memories of *Koshi*.

The first habitat the migrants reached was Garrigart a small desert town, where the Almonds and other migrants purchased bus tickets and boarded a bus to the coastal city of Zuluwarah all in Libya.

In this city, they spent weeks in a disused fish market that was bubbling with aspiring Europe-bound-migrant-day-dreamers. Highly skilled fake passport dealers made regular visits and were readily available with all the latest information updates on immigration formalities and migration routes to Europe and yonder. One, Antonio Gonzales, proudly displayed a letter of appreciation he had received from a migrant he had assisted to Hamburg. Scores of aspiring migrants converged to read Antonio's testimony letter.

Ali and her sisters carefully looked at the envelope. At the bottom of the sender's address was the inscription, 'Hamburg, Germany'. The content of the letter was rather short and read as follows:

'Thank you so much, Gonzales.

I spent two days in Yugoslavia, where I had good, beautiful Yugoslavian girls. I arrived in Hamburg airport safely. My passport was okay, and I was given a nice house to stay with a weekly allowance until my asylum case is sorted out. This is heaven on earth, very beautiful'.

Your friend,
Signed, Zerifu Keita of Hamburg

There was a surge towards Gonzales. Over twenty migrants signed up to take his route by air via Zagreb to Hamburg.

He seized the opportunity to inflate his charge, to the annoyance of his competitors.

Despite the inflated price of $600 each, the Almonds longed to go to Hamburg. But they were left with little cash, and they estimated that what they had wouldn't possibly be enough to carry three sisters through the entire journey.

They had only one option; they had to take the risk of selling some fake CFA francs in their possession.

Frances, the six foot five Senegalese immigrant who was a currency dealer walked into the market, along with his similarly sized entourage.

'Do you want dollars? How much do you want or have?' he asked.

'I have 50,000 CFA,' replied Ali.

'Okay, wait a moment,' Frances replied. He calmly shoved *Ali* aside, promising, 'I will be with you soon.'

'Hello!' Frances said as he moved leisurely towards Lokodiz, a Tunisian immigrant. 'Please take back your fake CFA money.' He stretched out his arm towards the Tunisian immigrant, holding the fake money out. 'And can I have my dollars back?' he demanded politely.

'Hey! What? Piss off. I don't have it. We had a deal right?' retorted Lokodiz angrily.

Two of Lokodiz's Tunisian mates joined in his defense.

'All right, this is your fake currency. I want my cash now,'

Frances reiterated calmly but with a frown.

Ali and her sisters took a step back, unable to believe the unfolding drama.

The three Tunisian migrants resisted.

Frances stepped back and soon returned with his entourage, totalling six men against three. Lokodiz and his compatriots, who had dominated a good number of disagreements, fought back, landing a few good jabs against the majority when the fighting first ensued.

However, the strain on their deficit soon netted results that came as no surprise. Within five minutes, Lokodiz and his two friends were bleeding profusely from their nostrils and gums.

Lokodiz groaned as he was pin to the ground. Frances, who was on top of him, squeezed his throat.

'Okay, okay!' Lokodiz managed to cry. 'Please, please—I beg your pardon. I will—I will give back your money!'

Frances let go of Lokodiz, and it was a shock to everyone to see how severely the Tunisian had been beaten within a matter of minutes. Lokodiz, trembling all over, hurriedly pulled down his trousers and brought out all the dollar bills he had bought with his fake currency.

'What a violent beating, '*Taba* whispered to *Ali*. 'Please, hide your currency. These giants would crush us if we messed with them,' she warned.

Out of apprehension, the sisters retreated with their notes, vowing never to bring them out; they could not possibly undergo such a rude beating if Frances were to detect that the money was fake.

'Hi, young man,' said Frances with a renewed smile as he walked towards *Ali*. 'How much did you say you want to change?'

'Er—we still haven't decided,' *Ali* replied, struggling to keep her composure. 'We will contact you later when we decide.'

Frances nodded with a smile and walked away, his associates, who looked like K-1 fighters, in tow.

Seven

The Almonds, having spent a week trying to figure out the cheapest move, gave up hope on Gonzales' trip due to insufficient funds.

Worse news soon came in. A joint EU patrol was about to launch operation 'Nautilus'. Word had it that a total of 115 boats, 25 helicopters, and 23 planes, plus a variety of other technical equipment, had been commissioned and would be patrolling the Mediterranean waters throughout the next month to prevent illegal migration. This was bad news for all the migrants, including the Almonds.

During the subsequent week, most of the migrants the sisters had travelled with had moved out of the area via Belgrade to Hamburg. The Almonds did not even have enough funds to make the cheapest move—a boat that would send them ahead to Italy.

By the third week, which came shortly, the sisters were devoid of any prospects or hope. They were totally stranded and completely out of cash. They woke to a strange spectacle.

The last fourteen migrants en route to Hamburg via Zagreb had been repatriated, and Gonzales was never seen again.

The following morning, on a Friday, while all were in grief, mourning their loss of hope and that they were stranded, two bulky-looking men wrapped in green turban veils walked in. *Ben* and her sisters' hearts leapt as the presence of the men brought back fresh memories of *Koshi*.

The men asked for everyone's attention in a rather polite way, to the surprise of the Almonds. An interpreter was sought.

'The market price for smuggling a person has dropped from $700 to $250, and this will be a special service day before Nautilus kicks off,' the men said.

Preparing for a temporary cessation of their activities, the smugglers had dropped their prices. They hoped to get more customers before their activities had to come to a halt. 'We are moving tomorrow; anyone who wants to sign up should pay by 7.00 p.m.,' they concluded.

And the rush for booking began.

'We have finally found an agent to convey us, and now we desperately need money to foot our bills. What do you think?' *Taba* said, confronting her sisters.

The situation compelled *Taba* to bring out the fake CFA francs, thinking of the much-needed U.S dollar.

'Sure, let's go for it,' *Ali* said.

Ben shook her head, denouncing the plan, but in the end she was compelled to approach the currency dealer.

She stood in front of two muscular men, including Frances.

She could hardly breathe as she looked at the men. They checked 'CFA', rubbing their hands over and over the notes before endorsing them, to her relief. She was given the CFA's equivalent in US dollars.

The next morning, in high hopes, all were busy making preparations for their departure.

Everything was calm among the migrants when a fellow migrant ran into the market. 'Something is going on,' he announced. 'There is a report of a lifeless body floating in the sea.' And subsequently, the man ran away.

The majority of the migrants followed him. He led them to the beach nearby, where they were confronted with a grisly scene. Standing on a dock, a local fisherman fished three corpses from the sea. Police officers were there, but they were not treating the deaths as suspicious. The place was the scene of such deaths, as the number of migrants riding on the Mediterranean waters had increased.

Ben, Ali, and *Taba* felt their confidence ebb away. But the incentive of getting to England made almost every migrant to relish the chance to stake a claim.

They were sneaked out onto the beach about eight miles away in groups of four, each group in turn lying flat on their backs in a Toyota pickup to avoid any possible detection, with the promised that, at dawn, they would certainly be conveyed to an Island in Italy. The agent and his mate left the migrants in the cold with the assurance, 'Stay here and don't panic.'

The migrants had already paid the smugglers, who promised to keep them near the shore until dawn. But when signs of daylight crawled in, no hope or sign of the boat had emerged.

Should we trek back to the town? Ben wondered. And then she thought, W*hat will befall us, supposing the driver fails to turn up?*

Similar thoughts plagued the minds of all who were stranded with the Almonds.

Their fears turned to joy when they caught a glimpse of the agent. 'There he is! The agent has fulfilled his promise!' *Ali e*xclaimed.

Hastily, the agent ordered all to get on board, an order with which the migrants complied, jumping into the boats with vigour. However, for the Almonds, it was a dreadful sight as they observed, for the first time in their lives, the lashing wind and the high tidal thump of the Mediterranean waves.

They were aided on board, as their fright seemed to paralyze them.

The estimated duration of the trip was four hours at most.

They would be ferried from the Libyan port of Zuwara under cover of darkness to the Italian port city of Sicily.

In total, twenty-two illegal immigrants, including the Almonds, found themselves cramped into a small wooden boat, powered by a rusty-looking Yamaha outboard motor.

They clung to each other for warmth.

With no navigational equipment, the two local captains depended heavily on luck to reach their target. As for the migrants, though wary of what lay ahead, they found the voice for a hearty conversation on board. They were in good spirits, with no doubts of seeing the shores of Europe soon.

Ishmael, who hailed from Egypt, was the first to show his determination despite the uncertainty that lay ahead. He said, 'I have tried to get into Spain from the fence between Morocco and Melilla more than ten times. This time, I need to succeed, so I changed my route.'

When *Ben* asked, 'Why are you still trying?' he answered simply. 'Ah, me?' He paused. 'For the same reasons you are.

'Back home, we are poor,' he lamented. 'We are faced with no jobs, adverse poverty, corrupt government. Look, I don't remember a single day that I didn't struggle to get food to eat. I am risking this journey for a better life for my family.'

No one spoke again for over an hour.

The boat drifted along calmly, with occasional ripples of debris picked up by the raging ocean. An hour and a half later, a foggy daylight brought hope that throbbed in the migrants' bosom's, but each felt like the ocean kept opening up, as if the water was being spit in volumes underneath the tiny boat. The hours kept adding up with no sign of an end.

The wind picked up and, in a short while, drove the cold through their jackets. Shortly, they faced the reality of what lay ahead as they huddled in the cold and the spray of sea water. Their situation worsened when they got drenched by intermittent drizzling rain.

With little warning, the outboard motor went dead.

'Oh my God,' the Egyptian lamented bitterly.

Presently, the seventh hour came to pass. Daylight was quickly diminishing and it would soon be night again, but the outboard motor failed to restart despite several attempts.

Everyone on board was speechless, with only one thing in mind—hope. But stories told by locals who objected to immigrants embarking on such perilous trips suddenly became present in their minds. 'The risk is not only about the high tidal waves,' the local warned, 'but of some surprising visitors—sharks.'

About sixteen species—some rumoured to be as long as ten meters—were believed to hunt freely in this part of the Mediterranean waters.

The boat was now completely at the mercy of the wind.

Awe-inspiring cliffs and traces of ancient shipwrecks loomed in the distance.

The desperation that had been long encroaching had dismantled their high hopes of seeing the shores of Sicily.

Suddenly a giant ugly vessel surfaced right in front of them.

'Oh Allah,' whispered one migrant.

It was a scene to stir fear into the hearts of even the most seasoned pirates. The Almonds cringed in fear and disbelief.

They had been blown off course and had been intercepted by Malta naval authorities.

Ishmael cursed himself for another failure. All were gripped with the distress of being sent back.

Meanwhile, Malta was struggling with migrants; reports suggested that the number of migrants arriving in Malta had more than tripled. Most of them, just as in the case of the Almond family, were blown off course or rescued at sea.

The migrants did not want to be in Malta, and Malta did not particularly want them.

However, luck was on their side, as Malta authorities were forbidden by international law to turn back distressed migrants in international waters; the country had an obligation to rescue them.

The twenty-two migrants, along with the Almonds, arrived in Malta and were escorted to a detention centre near Lyster Barracks in Valletta. It was quite late. The streets, though deserted, were lined with streetlights, to the excitement of the Almonds and the others.

Each migrant was handed a sheet entitled, 'Your rights and obligations', which none of the Almonds read. Most were surprised when they were searched and any cash found was confiscated. However, for the vast majority, the excitement of making a first step into Europe at least was more than enough. This led to some migrants abandoning their luggage and rushing to get mattresses at the detention centre.

The small room allocated to them at the centre was quite clean. It was lined with single beds in rows of twenty per room. They had a good night's sleep. For the Almonds, it was the first good night's sleep they'd had in months.

The next morning, the new migrants, including the Almonds, woke up to a spectacle they could hardly believe.

Their number of 22 had grown. They had joined an immigrant community of 628 people, bringing the total to 650, all held in the closed compound of the detention centre. A free newspaper for the detainees carried their story. Malta reported that a total of four boats, with around 100 immigrants on board, had been stopped by EU border vessels since the start of the Nautilus operation. Three of them had decided to continue on their journey to Malta and one of them to Italy's Lampedusa, as the guards were powerless to prevent this.

About 1.5 million migrants, although this figure was highly unreliable, made it into Europe illegally each year.

Migrating had become a way of life, commonly seen as life achievement among the poor immigrants' families. This popular mindset made the problem even more difficult; the motto was do or die.

According to statistics published, remittances sent home by sub-Saharan countries were estimated at more than $900 billion, almost one-third of those countries' budgets. And the figures were set to increase, as more migrants were on the move.

People in the detention centre couldn't get out. Because there were so many new migrants, some had to dwell in tents.

The next morning, all migrants gathered, awaiting a visit from Franco Frattini.

They were soon applauding, as the EU commissioner in charge of immigration issues took the stage to address them. He spoke at length, with great assurances. Due to a 'lack of adequate and available buildings', for now and into the immediate future, the situation was likely to continue, but the government would soon respond.

He soon waved to the migrants and left with his bodyguards.

The Almonds stood, not knowing exactly where to turn.

They paced forward, moving to their left, and stopped.

They stood as taut as piano wires, straining to catch sight of a friendly face.

Migrants from Afghanistan and Iraq made up the few females found among the predominant male Africans. Ben soon caught sight of a young woman cuddling an infant and a toddler, who both slept soundly. She was dressed in a Western outfit.

'Hey, this way,' Ben said moving toward the woman.

Ali and *Taba* doubled their pace in pursuit.

'Hello,' said Ben. 'Please, do you speak English?'

Her breath became heavier and her heartbeat doubled from the effort. But to the sister's great relief, she replied, 'Ah, yes.

Can I help you?'

The Almonds felt safer here in Malta and were less inclined to bother hiding their identities.

However, the three sisters maintained their boyish looks and responded swiftly to their male names. They wore baseball caps and sun shades all time. And they almost always allowed *Ali* to do the talking, for fear their voices might betray them.

'How long have you been in this detention centre?' *Ali* enquired.

'Um—Eleven months,' the woman replied.

The Almonds were not all that surprised when the husband,

Shayne, curiously hurried over and sat beside his wife.

'What?' *Ali* exclaimed. 'Why? Why so long?'

'My family and I don't want to be here. We hope to get to Italy,' the woman replied.

'We don't want to be here either,' replied *Ali*. 'We want to get to England.'

'Look,' the woman replied, pausing, 'I have to be honest with you. They don't want us to be here, and none of the migrants you see here want to be here.

'Even, last week, Valletta received international criticism for leaving twenty-seven shipwrecked Africans hanging onto tuna nets in the Mediterranean while arguing with Libya over who should pick them up. After three days, it was alleged that the Italian navy came to their rescue. In Italy, the treatment of immigrants is better, and the bonus is that the Italians give amnesty to illegal migrants more frequently.'

The Almonds and their newfound Iranian friends chatted at length. And as the days passed, the family got more acquainted but each rigidly shielded what had prompted their migration.

On the Almond's eighth day, a Sunday, the sisters and the Shayne family gathered together for their daily routine of marathon conversations, inspiring hope into each other.

Suddenly, Taba opened the lid on a question both families dreaded to ask each other.

'Please, er—' Taba hesitated and planted a finger into her mouth as a sign of regretting what she was about to ask. 'Why did you decide to make this journey with your children?'

Ali turned wordlessly in a disguised grimace to look at Taba in disapproval.

'We were a very happy family in Tehran,' Mr. Shayne began.

He spoke confidently, with a low, sometimes husky voice. 'I was an aircraft engineer. My salary was very good. But one morning, I was arrested, along with my wife. Due to her pregnancy, she was discharged soon afterwards, but she was always watched, always.'

Before Taba could interrupt, he continued.

'For adherence to our religious faith, I was arrested and jailed in Talishna, about 300 miles north of the Iranian capital, Tehran. After refusing to renounce my faith, I was placed in a solitary confinement for a year.'

He soon broke down in tears. He paused, wiped the tears from his eyes, and continued the narration. 'I was beaten and, look.' He took off his shirt calmly and showed his back to the Almonds. Multiple ragged coin-sized scars littered his back. These, he said, his interrogators had carved.

'I was repeatedly tied down, and each time a guard smoked, my back became the ashtray. They would yell at me to denounce my faith now or die.'

The emotions tugged fiercely at Shayne as re recounted what had happened, and he rose agitatedly to his feet. He paused and glanced around the room before sitting back down. 'For them, it was a great fun. I saw an opportunity one day, and I managed to escape with my family, hoping to get to Western Europe to seek asylum.

'Officials at the office of the UN High Commissioner for Refugees in Van Eastern Turkey say the number of Iranian asylum seekers, including those from my religious group, has steadily risen over the last three years. Nearly half of those granted refugee status last year in Italy were from my tribe, so we are hoping to succeed,' he concluded.

For the first time since they had left home, the Almonds were compelled to share their secret. Hastily, *Ben* explained who they were and the sort of trouble that had befallen them thus far. They suddenly realized that going forward from that detention centre would be another hurdle.

Eight

Soon the days turned to weeks and months. Occasionally new faces arrived at the centre. Some were being sent back after their request for asylum had failed. And each day, the migrants became depressed as mates were hauled away for deportation. As the day went by, each feared he or she would soon be the next to go.

One wonders how, within confinement, agents could still infiltrate. It was without much difficulty that the Almonds found themselves presented with an alternative means for leaving, and they were intrigued, since they knew that their request for asylum would likely fail.

At dawn one morning, a terrified twenty-four-year-old burst into tears as news of his rejected asylum request and subsequent deportation reached him. He revealed how others could buy their way out of the detention centre.

Following the directions and help of that inmate, the Almond sisters made it out of the centre to meet a Mr Tuavaree, a Maltese who secretly shipped illegal immigrants to their desired destinations. Agents such as Mr Tuavaree knew exactly which passports were exempt from visas in any part of the developed world.

At the smuggler's doorstep, the sisters paused, shocked by the fiercely huge size of Mr Tuavaree. They stood for a few seconds staring in amazement, to the annoyance of the man.

'Hey!' he yelled in utmost disrespect. 'What do you want?'

He raced towards them.

Ben quickly recovered from her slumber and answered,

'Please, sir, we just been directed to see you in order to make a move, and we prefer the United Kingdom.'

'Fine,' the big man answered. 'Have a seat,' he added.

'You would need Bahamas passports, or if you are not confident about your ability to pass as Bahamian, you can go for the easier one, err—Guinea, I mean Papua New Guinea. That will be $200 each.'

That would mean another journey by sea, and the sister would genuinely have loved to decry the notion—surely there must be another option. But at least the prospect would keep their dreams alive.

The Almonds each acquired a Guinea passport, and they were amazed and delighted with how perfect the passports looked. Their boyish images fit perfectly in the spot for the passport holder's photo. And in no time, the sisters were being conveyed speedily towards the Grand Harbour.

Long chimneys of giant fleets emerged in the distance as they approached the harbour. At the mouth, they observed a lot of fortifications facing northeast on both sides and countless vessels at berth at the wharf. Bounded to the north was St Elmo's Point, also berthed with various vessels.

The *Catania* was marked in bold script. Next to it was the *Akula* and *Celtic Mariner*.

Some vessels were further away and sheltered by an isolated breakwater, which was largely covered by the city of Valletta and its suburb, Floriana. This peninsula also divided Grand Harbour from a second parallel natural harbour.

The Shaynes turned forty the next month. Tuavaree's policy was to recruit only younger migrants and to avoid all together women and children. Even the acquisition of passports and heaps of persuasion would not make him rethink. Thus, to the sadness of the Almond's, the Shaynes were disqualified from being smuggled on board the giant cargo vessels bound for the United Kingdom via France.

The sisters, along with Tuavaree and a new group of immigrants, proceeded to a bunch of busy men loading fishmeal onto the *Akula*.

"Each of you is to take one of these bags and follow right behind me. But wait," said Tuavaree. He took a few steps away from the migrants, who were six in all, including the Almonds. The three others were Chinese immigrants from the southeastern Fujian Province.

When Tuavaree returned, he introduced a lanky-looking man in his late thirties. 'This is Antonio, and he will take care of you on board.'

'Okay,' whispered Antonio, "since the attacks of 11 September 11 2001, it has become more difficult to be a stowaway onboard transportation arriving to or departing from Western European. Port security has drastically increased, and among the new security measures, security watches over crew members as they load, at which time stowaways usually comingle with the crew to gain entrance into ships.' He paused and briefly squeezed his nose.

'Anyway,' he said, 'I will lead you on board, but we have to disguise each of you as loaders, so please each carry a bag and come with me. No questions, okay?'

'Er—Lest I forget,' murmured Tuavaree to Antonio. Both men moved aside and spoke in a low tone, to the discomfort of the Almonds. 'I I want nothing to impede us; I mean nothing,' they heard Tuavaree warn.

It was a difficult task for the Almonds to try to come to terms with taking another sea voyage. Taba in particular was unable to hide her fears. She approached Antonio and asked, 'Are we safe?'

'Of course yes. Why do you ask?'

'Er—you know, stories of stowaways being killed or thrown overboard, right?' Taba managed.

Antonia laughed her concerns off, saying, 'Among ways for refugees to seek passage to the West, stowing away on a Western-flagged ship can be an effective and comfortable way to gain entry into the United Kingdom, due to the strict humanitarian codes observed on all the developed Western countries' vessels.'

The ship had multiple compartments, so the migrants were split into two groups of three. Each group was hidden separately within the second cargo hold beneath the very lowest compartment of the *Akula*, an Antigua and Barbuda-flagged shipping vessel. Hidden within the fishmeal, the refuges were warned, 'Dare not let yourselves out until the ship docks, and when these mills are being taken out, you guys must blend up and each carry a bag and find your way out, all right?'

They all remembered being told that the journey should take about six and a half hours. Each migrant was hidden away from the others, but none needed to be told that his or her companions weren't far off as, together but separately, they felt the movement of the ship gliding on the water, bound for a route from the Mediterranean Sea through the Suez Canal and into the Red Sea.

*   *   *

Taking comfort in Antonio's assurances of safety, Taba sneaked out of her hiding place when she estimated that five hour had elapsed. She needed some water and nonchalantly wandered onto the upper deck.

Two crew members sharing a bottle of whisky below the superstructure yelled at Taba as they caught sight of her. A third approached, and Taba recognized him as Antonio.

Taba smiled and walk towards him. 'I need some water please,' she said.

Racing at her, Antonio roared, 'Who the fuck are you? And how the hell did you get on board?" He showed no remorse or sign of recognition in his angry retort.

Taba's heart sank. She turned away to retreat, but Antonio, who was closest to her, had caught her by the arm.

'Bring him down here,' said one of the crew members. 'Give him something as a souvenir.'

'You are right, Kuala, but how?' replied the other.

The men thought for a few moments. *Taba*, relieved over the mention of a souvenir, again reiterated her desire for water.

'Bring him down here,' said Kuala, savouring the words as they formed inside his aching head. 'Throw him overboard.'

Taba, immediately choked with horror, started screaming.

She clung with one hand to Antonio's shirt, while her other fingers clawed at the rear rail of the ship.

Taba was horrified as Antonio started dragging her by the feet; he was soon joined by Kuala and two other sailors.

Taba was being pushed to the edge, and with a splash, she had been thrown into the wild ocean.

She was going down fast. She sucked in some water and began sputtering. The water was salty. She tried not to open her mouth for another taste, but her shortness of breath forced her mouth open. She felt the salty water trickling into her mouth and down her resisting throat and lungs.

It is very dark down here, she thought wearily. She fought against the darkness. Her feet never touched the bottom.

She pushed hard, and her head rose above the water. She caught a quick glimpse of the ship far ahead. Unable to sustain herself, she went down again.

She fought vainly over overwhelming odds. After four minutes, her splashing and exertions died out. Her hope of reaching the shores of Europe ended in the deep ocean.

*   *   *

The ship docked, and each of the remaining migrants managed to make their way safely out. Ali and Ben waited in vain for Taba. The situation compelled the two sisters to storm the ship in search of their sister. Both sister, as if possessed, became less mindful of being arrested and stormed every corner of the cargo ship in search of their sister. Ali yelled over and over for Taba; only her own voice echoed back to her ears. They wandered around the port, not even knowing which country they were in.

'Ah,' *Ali* whispered as she caught sight of Antonio.

Both sisters raced towards him. 'Have you seen *Taba*?' Ali asked. 'I mean one person among us is missing.'

Antonio turned, looked at the sisters and the tree Chinese migrants. 'Long gone,' he said simply and walked away.

The sisters sensed an expression of an unspoken fear on Antonio's face.

Nine

Ali and Ben feared the worse but could not confirm their fears; they were confused and their thoughts highly dismantled. Somehow, they managed to make their way out of the port. They held out hope that *Taba* might be alive somewhere.

Once they started to take in their surroundings, *Ben* and *Ali* noticed that the people here had a strange way of dressing, one that was quite similar to the garb in their native Somalia. The men wore kurta, a loose-fitting shirt that fell below the knees traditionally worn by Muslim men. And the few women the Almonds could see were in the most visible form of the hijab. Ali and Ben were alarmed, as the hijabs went beyond the head scarf; the veils completely covered the women. Only their hands, faces, and feet were not covered by the loose, non-see-through garments.

'This language can't be English, can it?' Ben asked softly.

The words they heard around them didn't even sound close to English.

'And it can't be French either,' Ali whispered.

In hushed tones, both sisters acknowledged, 'This can't be England.'

Ali saw a sign that read, 'Welcome to the Al Wajh, the Republic of Arabia.'

The girls could not believe what they had just read; they stood speechless, their jaws dropped.

Al Wajh was a coastal town in north-western Saudi Arabia on the coast of the Red Sea. It was part of the Tabuk Province of the Kingdom of Saudi Arabia. It was a comparatively small town, whose citizens were mainly of Al Belawi, Al Huety, and Al Johani tribes. The natives fished and did peasant farming. A road closely linked Al Wajh with the city of Tabuk. The port, which used to be one of the main ports in the region fifty years ago, was mainly used for fishing.

'What?' *Ben* murmured.

The girls had no clue what was going on. *Ali* questioned herself over and over again. *How did the ship stray?*

She burst into tears for the first time during the entire journey. She had been able to resist shedding tears so as not to discourage her sisters, even when they had lost little *Koshi*. But the realization that their situation had not gotten any better and the thought that something evil might have befallen *Taba* made her unable to control her tears.

This day, February 28, marked exactly one year since the Almonds embanked on their journey to Europe, and it coincided with the, Liberation of Kuwait. Codenamed

Felix Kobla Wornameh

Operation Desert Storm commonly referred to as simply the Gulf War, was a war waged by a U.N.-authorized coalition force from 34 nations led by the United States, against Iraq in response to Iraq's invasion and annexation of Kuwait

The girls' misery was compounded when they were told that, due to the liberation, there had been civil unrest in the locality, prompting authorities to impose a dawn to dusk curfew and they were twenty minutes away from being caught breaking the law. The usual smile of the Almonds was long forgotten as they faced the rigid reality of their situation.

They spoke to anyone who would listen, desperately seeking a place to lodge. No one showed them compassion, as the locals hastily finished their work to escape the ring of the siren. They felt sick to their stomachs as the many doors were shut in their faces each time they asked for help. The inability to communicate made the situation even more frustrating for them.

They wandered about aimlessly, noticing the occasional sneering looks from the locals. They came to a halt near a mosque with a clock tower. *Ali*, in apprehension, hastily glanced at the tower clock—6.50. 'We have only ten minutes left,' she lamented bitterly to *Ben*. 'What shall we do now?'

Ben hesitated awhile and said, 'Let's get into this mosque and pass the night there. What do you think?'

Ali's thoughts raced, and she did not answer. Rather, she approached a young man sprinting by; with little hesitation, *Ali* addressed the young man in a Somali language.

He stopped in his tracks and responded in a clear Somali language, to the joy of the dismayed Ali and Ben.

Both sisters, wiping tears from their eye, announced their predicament. Without hesitation, the young man ordered them to race and follow him. He led them on for about four minutes through some narrow alleys, passed about seven bakeries, and to a dilapidated mud structure. He stopped at the entrance and banged at a steel gate. The rusted steel door hissed noisily as it was held open by two young men. 'Hi, Abdullah, these guys—Er—they just arrived.' Upon saying those words, the young man turned and ran, disappearing deep into the alleys.

The sisters were offered a cup of water to calm their nerves.

After that, Abdullah spelt out the laws governing the ghetto.

The first was the most alarming one. 'Do not ever run in here if you are chased from outside by immigration or the police.

'Point number two,' he continued. 'Do not dare to come into this ghetto for your belongings if you are caught and subject to deportation.' He concluded by saying, 'Do not dare sleep in this ghetto if you fail to honour a day's payment.'

These words never stopped ringing in the two sisters minds until they had finally fallen asleep in the 20-millimetre square that had come, temporarily, into their possession.

Because of the pay-per-night system, Ben woke up the following morning to see every immigrant hastily preparing to go out for the day's struggle to find wages.

Ben got her sister's attention and, after they had hastily acquainted themselves with the others, the Almonds joined the company of refugees as they headed out for the day.

They trekked for about two miles away from the ghetto into the heart of the small city of Al Wajh.

Finally, they perched along the road, waiting for the relatively random casual employers. With no guarantee that someone would need their services, they patiently waited and hoped.

The day's hope soon diminished, and all reassembled in the ramshackle ghetto. The population seemed huge for such a small house, but who dared to question this ghetto boss.

'Everyone is allocated a space the size of his body; it is virtually impossible to turn one's body while sleeping. Your only option is to get up, turn to your desired position, and lie still again,' said Bo, a pale-looking Pilipino immigrant.

The Almonds took possession of the little corner assigned to them; to ward off the cold, they clung to each other as they slept.

Day two saw almost everyone out looking for a job in the tiny village. Only the few who had some money left on them proceeded on their journey, hoping to reach the capital city of Riyadh.

Al Wajh, being one of the remotest villages in Arabia, offered the refugees no way of surviving, other than to look for jobs from the fishermen at the port or from the peasant farmers.

The harbour, which could have been a better option for finding menial jobs, became a no-go area when news of an immigration swoop reached the ghetto.

One way or the other, the stranded migrants boosted the labour market. Locals used the opportunity and exploited the refugees, paying very little for a lot of work.

Ben and Ali lived in perpetual fear of being exposed as females. The consequences of that in an Arab world were unimaginable. They chose to almost always move together.

Ben's first attempt to get a job was not successful. Though she initially got the job, she was rejected for being too feeble and because she could not walk without limping from previous exertions. The disguised sisters could only watch, numb, hoping that someone would hire their services.

Those who had the advantage over the Almonds had a good meal provided by their employer. The Almonds' throats watered at the news. They had not had a decent meal in months. The only consolation they had was to cover another seven kilometre journey on foot and back to get bread from a bakery.

Ben's first day at work was a novelty. A pickup car came to a halt at a distance. All the men raced for it, but the disguised sisters remained behind, too scared to make the run.

Ben managed some confidence and followed. The car suddenly sped off again. All the men puffed on, reaching the car when it stopped for the second time. About seven young men, including *Ben*, boarded. Soon, the driver came

and ordered some of the men down. He made his selection based on physique.

The driver assessed Ben, and though he had no doubt or suspicions about her gender, her feeble physique made her an undesirable worker. The man asked Ben to get down.

She refused and burst into tears. She was too desperate for a job. All efforts by the man to get rid of Ben, even with the backing he had from other migrants, were fruitless.

She strangely resisted all attempts to exempt her from the chosen squad. The tears continued rolling down her cheeks.

As if to avoid hurting her any more, the employer decided to keep her among the crew and drove off to the farm.

Meanwhile, Ali, typically the extrovert among the Almonds, for some reasons could not overcome the loss of Taba and could still not bring herself to terms with their new environment.

*   *   *

The temporarily recruited migrants, including Ben, were speedily conveyed in a Peugeot 404 pickup to a farm on the outskirts of town.

The employer explained the day's job. 'You are to use spades to dig out the moist earth from this old trench,' he said.

Scarcely had the migrants started this tedious job when the employer realized the agility in *Ben's* feeble body. The man asked 'the boy's' name.

'Ahmed is my name,' *Ben* lied, thinking that, after all, these people really preferred Muslims.

In the afternoon, the workers were brought rice with a delicious tomato sauce. It was *Ben's* first meal in weeks. She ate till her stomach could take no more.

*   *   *

'At the end of the job, he gave us two dinners each. To me, it was my happiest day since I embarked on this journey,' said *Ben* happily to her sister, who, for the first time, responded positively.

On their way to the usual job centre the following day, *Ben* overheard a name being called out. 'Ahmed! Ahmed!'

A few seconds passed before the name suddenly jogged her memory and she realized the person was calling for her. It was the employer who she'd worked for the previous day.

She galloped towards him, and both sisters were taken in his car to the 'labour market', where the migrants usually assembled to look for jobs. There, Ben found she had the privilege to choose work, as the farmer had deemed her capable of doing a good job, and thus, she was able to draft her sister without question from the employers.

Being children of peasant farmers, the Almonds did not detest physical labour. They fit perfectly well within the jigsaw puzzle they had found themselves in. They soon became the toast of the farmers in the community, partially due to the seriousness and a touch of class they added to the jobs. They always worked hard and stringently refused to talk in the midst of a job.

The Almonds access to jobs became easier than it was for most of their male colleagues, despite the large number of stranded immigrants. What they normally received as rewards for their jobs wasn't enough, as they had to pay every night at their place of abode. This pay-per-day method made things very difficult for many of the refugees, including the Almonds, who needed to save towards their journeys, for which they would have to pay up front.

* * *

Although the sisters could not explain how they'd ended up in Arabia, they still maintained the hope that they would make it to the United Kingdom one day. And they knew that it was important for them to stop lamenting over having been deceived again.

After a day's work on a Thursday afternoon, at approximately 4.50 p.m., *Ben* and *Ali* strolled the deserted 44b Moro street leading to their home.

'If we can keep getting jobs here and not be discovered, we can save and fly out to London some day, right?' *Ali* said, trying to sound assuring. 'Ben?'

Ben made no sound but nodded her head in approval.

Just then, a grey Peugeot 505 screeched to a halt beside them. The driver's side window lowered, and a man in his mid-thirties wearing a turban smiled at them. They smiled back. He asked if they were closed for the day.

'Not at all,' Ali replied.

Ben quickly opened the door, as this was the normal way of accepting a job.

'No, no,' the man protested. 'I need only one person for a little ironing job.'

Both sisters, unwilling to let go, tried to convince each other to give up the job. 'Look, you made more money today than me,' Ali claimed. 'Let me have this one.'

'All right, you.' In the end, the man pointed at Ali.

Ben walked away alone but continued to turn back enviously to watch the speeding car until it disappeared from her sight. 'I spotted the customer first. I should have gotten that job,' she murmured to herself as she made her way home.

Ten

Back in the ghetto, Ben waited for her sister to return.

They both usually showered together so that they could keep watch for one another. Three hours passed, and *Ali* had not returned.

*   *   *

The grey Peugeot 505 sped past the town centre onto an isolated stretch of road. It took a sharp left off the tarred road into the desert. *Ali's* heartbeat raced as the man continued to drive deep into the desert.

Ali thought of asking the man where they were going, but each time she looked at the man intending to ask the question, the man responded with a warm smile. 'Okay, no worry.'

Finally, he pulled over at a disused farm shelter; he vacated his front seat and gazed around for a few seconds then returned to the back seat, where *Ali* sat nervously. The man started to undress himself and bid her to get closer.

Oh my god! She is a woman, Ali gasped to herself.

Having revealed her identity, the woman, pleaded, 'Please, I have longed for a man all these years. Don't worry. Just hurry up, and I will pay $100.' With that, she started to undress in front of the trembling Ali.

Ali was too terrified to utter a word. She cast her mind back to an account of a migrant who claimed he had been raped by a woman at gunpoint—a rumour she had long forgotten. She had worn a frown in disbelief of her fellow migrant's assertion.

It had been alleged that woman in Arabia who passed the average marriage age scarcely get husbands and were forbidden to marry a non-Muslim, let alone a foreigner.

So these unfortunate women often had no choice but to remain single for life and could not indulge in any kind of intimacy. For some of the desperate ones, the only way to curb their sexual desires was to secretly rape innocent migrants.

This woman, whom Ali had never set eyes on before, became alarmed at Ali's lack of effort. 'Come on,' she screeched. As the command issued this command, she, to Ali's surprise, brandished a short gun, pointing at Ali as she uttered a few words in Arabic—' Do it or die' Ali presumed.

Ali managed to look into the woman's eyes, and she saw the threat of her worsening anger. The woman's face had turned from pale to purple, and her eyes appeared reddish and bulged larger than normal. *Ali* could see nothing but terror in those eyes.

What can I do now? she thought wearily. She tried to say a word but felt as if her jaws had been clamped shut. She grew more frightened and confused as the woman held the gun against her head.

In one last act of defiance, *Ali* held her breath and shut her eyes Brief seconds later, she felt her heartbeat sink as the gun clicked. Subsequently, the woman struck her with the back of the gun. The blow was hard, but luckily *Ali* only sustained blisters on her lower lips. The woman pushed her out of the car and sped off without further utterance.

Ali wandered about until she made her way back into town. She arrived at the ghetto late in the night.

'What kept you so long?' Ben asked agitatedly, unable to wait for her sister to explain herself. 'I have been waiting to have a shower; shall we?'

Ali made no sound but slumped into her bed. She scratched her head for a while before giving an account of her dangerous adventure.

The thought of the day's ordeal was so fresh on her mind that she couldn't manage to sleep properly. On this day, they were exactly two years into their journey to Europe and a year into their lodging in the ghetto of Al Wajh.

Ben, very unusually, awoke in the middle of the night and decided to visit the pit latrine.

Adjacent to this latrine were three small single rooms occupied by three immigrant couples. The rooms were generally, if not always, shut during the day. But the door was open at that time of the night, and four uniformed policemen walked in, followed by a fifth in plain clothes.

The frightened Ben, retreated and, waiting in her corner, watched on.

The three husbands came out simultaneously to meet the strangers. They shook hands and whispered a few words to each other. Much to *Ben's* surprise and relief, she seemed to be observing a cordial relationship. There was a quick change of hands, but *Ben* could not imagine what the officers had placed in the palms of the husbands. Whatever they had received, each man had immediately tucked it into his wallet.

Could it be drugs? she wondered.

She turned around to go get her sister, but on second thought, realized her movement through the packed room might wake people.

All of a sudden, three of the uniformed policemen reclined their rifles by the door entrance and walked into a room each. Then the doors shut consecutively.

The officers who remained behind looked relaxed but slightly agitated. They gazed frequently around the compound as they lit a tobacco pipe and chatted in very discreet tones, smiling as they spoke.

Ben was welled hidden. She heard no noise, except the unceasing sounds of multiple people snoring in the dark packed room.

About fifteen minutes passed. The middle door opened, and the man came out of the room. He looked around very suspiciously. Then, zipping his trousers up, he gave a thumbs up to his companions in the middle room. They smiled back, and the man beamed with look of gratitude.

After a short while, the next door on the left also opened, and another uniformed policeman walked out in a similar fashion.

The strange scene became clear to Ben when each outgoing man was replaced by one of the two awaiting men and the door shut behind him.

Finally, each door opened and shut for the last time. The man in mufti, who was slightly fat with a protruding pot belly, kicked the air in joy and glanced around again in the dark.

The officers assembled, tucked in their uniforms properly, and took custody of their guns. All took a final look around suspiciously to make sure no one had seen them. They had no clue that *Ben* was watching.

Ben's mind was locked on the scene until the crack of dawn, when she finally fell fast asleep.

She was awakened shortly by *Ali* yelling at her. 'Hey! What's wrong with you today?' *Ali* demanded. 'Wake up. We're going to be late.'

'Hmm,' *Ben* responded, unable to open her eyes; rather, she repositioned herself, pulled a ragged leftover blanket over her head, and soon regained a full slumber, to the annoyance of her sister.

'Guess who came here? The mudee came looking for us,' Ali told her sister, referring to the man for whom *Ben* had worked that first day.

The mention of the boss forced *Ben* awake. She hurriedly pulled the blanket from her face and sprang nimbly to her feet. Gaping around, she rubbed her eyes to get rid of the sleepiness.

She splashed some chilled water over her head, and since they always slept with their clothing on, Ben was soon walking down the road with Ali.

'Where is the mudee? Did he really come?' she enquired.

'Yes,' Ali replied. 'He really did stop by the ghetto asking after Ahmed, but I guess he was only passing by; maybe he just wanted to check on you to see if you were doing all right.'

'Okay, fine,' Ben answered sharply.

'What do you think about our continued stay in that polluted ghetto?' Ali asked.

'What else can we do? Do you have any other ideas?'

'Well, I met some guys yesterday who left the ghetto,' her sister answered.

'And where are they staying?' asked Ben. 'Is it cheaper?'

'In the dense hedges near the Kalifu mosque. Um—' Ali hesitated. 'They told me there is a risk the ghetto will soon be raided by the immigration authorities. It may happen any night.'

'Do you believe that?' *Ben* asked swiftly.

'Maybe,' *Ali* replied. 'They raided the harbour area last night again, and the occupants of Kurasa ghetto were all busted and deported.'

'I don't care. At this point, I'd even prefer being deported home. I am sick and tired of this life. I—' *Ben* stammered and her voice became very low. 'I even wish I was dead.'

Ali looked at her sister sternly for a few seconds and then asked softly, 'How can you say that?'

Ben made no response.

'Hey! Look at me.' *Ali* held her sister close. 'If we go back now, we will have no recognition. Who do we have to stand for us? Did you think about this?'

After a brief silence, *Ben* spoke. 'I saw something last night.'

'What was it?' Ali asked.

'I think those couples in the ghetto came here for business,' her sister replied, looking away.

'I don't understand. What exactly do you mean?' Ali pressed.

Ben explained what she'd seen. 'They were uniformed policemen. I think those couples only pretend. In reality, they are whores, and their husbands solicit male customers to sleep with their wives for cash.'

The story came as no surprise to Ali, as she had long heard rumours circulating about every migrant couple in town. But she was concerned to hear about the police involvement. That meant the ghetto would be a target; raid on prostitution always remained inevitable.

The sisters, realizing the risk involved, made up their minds to move out of the ghetto as soon as possible.

That evening, the Almonds paid their ghetto arrears and demanded their passports, which, according to the rules of the ghetto, the landlord held.

Four other friends from the ghetto also shared similar concerns, so the six refugees teamed up.

The Almonds together with the others marched towards the principal's door. Muamah Muambah, is the person having the prime responsibility of the ghetto. He is a fellow migrant from Eritrea who preferred to be called Principal for no apparent reason.

The group, wary that decisions to move out of a ghetto could be a dangerous one, held their breath at the door.

It had been alleged that an Albanian immigrant was tortured and killed back in 1998 for wanting to swap ghettos. His murder sparked outrage but, no one was held responsible.

In spite of the wariness, Ashanti, a chubby looking young man among the group managed a wry smile.

"I'm sure we are all nervous?" He said as he directed his rare smiles towards the group A feeble looking Bulgarian reddened on the face retorted angrily "What do you mean? Anyway, I am not."

It is typical of the Almonds not to utter a word when in the midst of other migrants. They refrain making comment.

Ali knocked on the door.

The principal called them in "come on, stand in line". He smile and seemed to be enjoying his authority as he observed the group shuffle slowly into line.

He then asked of their mission but no one among the group was willing to talk. In the end, Ali, uncomfortable about the growing tension broke the silence. Aware of what could happen she thought carefully and phrased the sentence in the best possible manner. "We please want our passports back to enable us move to the big city."

For a few moments, he only looked at the group with a suspicious smile and said nothing. He then sighed audibly in the end and said" stay here this place is a big city too"

"No please we want the passport" Ali answered sharply

The fact that Ali was logicaly right to demand her passport only made matters worse. Muamba the principal, just like other ghetto leaders constantly opt for physical means as the way of solving problems. He sprung onto his feet and snorted "you are going to either change your mind or, I will turn your life in this city inside out." He back sat inclined to his chair watching TV.

Ali without hesitation, reiterated calmly "please give us our passports now" unfortunately, *Ben* could not refrain from talking, she added, "We need the passports now!"

Muambah's face grimaced and he started to rise from his seat.

He grabbed *Ali* by the shirt. When she tried to walk away, he pushed her back at which time she hit her head against the adjoining wall, "Stop it" her sister yelled at him Principal then asked everyone to leave the room; the group shuffled and slowly move out except the two sisters who chose to stay in the room for their passport.

Muamba, inches away from their face, taunted them "I will teach you two guys a lesson, I will show you that I have lived in this city long enough to be respected"

The poor girls uttered no word. He dashed back to a closet nearby and collected some passports and aggressively pushed the sisters out throwing the passports at them.

They swiftly picked their passports and luckily for the others in the group their passports were among. They were glad and made their way out of sight hurriedly.

About nine ghettos were scattered across the township, each segregated along racial lines. For example, the Shanghai ghetto was heavily dominated by the Chinese and some Burmese and other Far East Asians, while the Marati ghetto was mostly made up of the Indians and the Bangladeshis.

Eleven

With none of the other ghettos in their favour, the six refugees were compelled to seek refuge in hedges near the mosque where they usually stood in search of jobs. The place exposed them to the cold desert wind, but, highly determined to save money, they used this place as their bedroom for several days.

The new, unusual habit soon became normal. They perfected their ability to creep into the hedges late at night, avoiding been seen and crept out very early before daylight had taken over the dark. Since there was no form of bathing, they usually washed only their heads and faces, and the Almonds had to take advantage of very unusual hours to take care of additional hygiene.

For three weeks in succession, the nights in these hedges were tolerable and peaceful, except for the cold. Then one night, which happened to be very cold, the unexpected happened. They had just fallen asleep, when they heard strange noises in the distance, followed by a sound that they could distinguish as a gunshot.

Each migrant hastily raised his or head and searched around for the enemies' approach. They heard more of the same sounds, amid pattering footsteps that seemed to be closing in on them. They hastily got up on their knees. While *Ali* looked over *Ben's* left shoulder, her sister looked in the opposite direction.

So they could listen more attentively and with eager looks, the other migrants sprang to their feet and were soon in full flight, uttering lamentable cries. 'Yala, we are in trouble.'

'It's the police,' voices cried.

Ali and Ben followed in the tracks of the other refugees. They covered close to four hundred meters in darkness, falling over and over again, due to the uneven nature of the ground. They at last become conscious that no one was chasing them after all. Sneaking back in the darkness, they found that what they'd heard was only a faulty car; they raised quite loud peals of laughter.

For all these days sleeping in the hedges, Ali could think of nothing other than how and when they would raise enough money to make the journey to the capital city or to any other well-developed city in Arabia.

After nearly a year and a half of assiduous labour in Al Wajh, the sisters, along with twelve young men, boarded a bus bound for the central city of Riyadh. But soon after the bus had taken off, it was checked at a police barrier. Thus, all fourteen were ejected.

The bus fare was not refunded. With their heads sinking to their bosoms and their eye cast upon the ground, the migrants took the road back in despair. Others who made similar efforts were also thrown out of the bus, making it extremely difficult for them to get transport to proceed on their journey.

Looking for alternatives, they found the opportunity to pay a man to sneak them through. In no time, they did what was needed. They negotiated a fare and set off.

This time, they found themselves again in a Peugeot pickup.

Again, they were ordered to lie on their backs to avoid being seen. They, of course, complied with this instruction without hesitation.

After a short drive, the pickup came to a halt; the migrants maintained their position in silence. Their chests heaved up and down, betraying their nervousness as they overheard what seemed a marathon conversation between what *Ali* and the rest perceived to be the police and the driver.

A human shadow fell over *Ben*, and she heard a cry. 'Come down.'

In a mournful silence, all rose to their feet and climbed down from the truck to behold three young men in military uniform.

'Come over here!' one of the men ordered.

'Form a queue,' added another.

The migrants hastily obeyed. Every migrant was whipped violently, to the extent that the Almonds' eyes quickly shed tears.

After taking a great deal of delight in assaulting the weary refugees, the youngest among the uniformed men yelled, 'Get seated on the floor. I say sleep on the ground!' He made them lie on their backs, facing the sun.

His other colleagues ordered the driver to vacate the scene, which he did in haste.

Three to four hours later they were loaded into a military truck. They were driven miles away and dumped on a settlement farm, where the ardent rays of the sun failed to revive their hopes.

The assumption that the refugees would become trapped in tedious farm jobs was why the military took them there.

Late in the evening, the two sisters sneaked to the roadside.

Luckily, they found a lift back.

Not willing to give up, they found another driver who was willing to sneak some migrants through. 'I can easily take you through without any trouble,' the driver assured them.

'Look, I am a soldier myself, so don't worry!'

The spirits of most of the migrants trying to move out were very low, but that last tidbit pleased them exceedingly.

This time around, the journey commenced in the night.

But they had not quite covered six kilometres, when they noticed that a Toyota Land Cruiser seemed to be pursuing them. To be sure of this, the driver diverted off the road and headed into the desert.

To their surprise, the Land Cruiser followed in hot pursuit.

In terror, the driver doubled his speed. He made a sudden halt near some scattered rocks and cried out, 'Get down!

Run away quickly. Hurry; it's the police!'

Ali and the others jumped from the car in haste. They quickly took a drink from their clutched gallons of spring water and thus refreshed, headed out into the desert. They couldn't imagine what would befall them if they were caught. And endeavouring to avoid whatever punishment awaited them, they tracked deep into the desert, stopping only to catch their breaths.

When they finally regrouped and worked up the courage to walk back to the roadside, neither their driver nor their tormentor were anywhere to be found. They had been robbed yet again of transportation.

This unceasing frustration dispelled the hopes of some of the migrants, among them Lucy, a Vietnamese female who had became close friends of the Almonds. She decided to relinquish further undertakings and make her life in Al Wajh.

Lucy was a very attractively-looking girl, but she wobbled awkwardly on her right foot when she walked. She was in her early twenties and spoke of how her husband, Mr Min Lieu, misled her into Al Wajh.

'My husband lived here for four years before coming back to Vietnam to pick me up, and he promised that a better life awaited me here,' she had told the sisters. She'd paused and added, 'My husband forced me to sleep with people as a job. He threatened me so I obeyed.'

Luckily, her husband had been arrested in the harbour raid the previous month. Hence, Lucy was free. 'I want to go back to Vietnam after I work and save some money,' she confided. She paused briefly before adding, 'But my husband and I suffered a lot to get here.'

Ali and Ben quietly looked at each other without uttering a word but were satisfied to have confirmation of their suspicion.

'Look,' Lucy said, pulling up her trousers to display a deep scar under her ankle. 'My husband and I were stranded in Shubha sharing a ghetto like this one. Lieu used a matchstick he found on the kitchen table to light the gas stove. One of the managers walked into the kitchen and, without uttering a word, he picked the matchbox up and turned it over'.

'He then cried out, "Who asked you to use my matchstick?"

'Lieu was taken by surprised. He stood still for a moment, at a loss as to what to say. "Please," he said, after he had regained his composure, "I am sorry for not asking you."

'The manager roared and went on, "If you don't want trouble, then quickly pay five dollars!"

'We couldn't really tell if he meant what he'd said. So my husband asked, "Did you say five dollars?"

'"Yes!" the manager yelled at the top of his voice. "You heard me right!"

'Lieu was asked horrified at the demand. Even though he was an illegal alien, he decided to fight for his rights. "How can I pay a whole five dollars for a matchstick?" he demanded.

"A whole packet is worth less than half a dollar."

'The ghetto manager was soon joined by his deputy, and the two of them became highly agitated over my husband's wise words. One of them threw the matchbox at his face.

He avoided it and braced for a struggle. I was shocked to see my husband on top of these guys within minutes of the brawl.'

Both *Ali* and *Ben* cried and clasped Lucy's hands in praise of her courageous story.

She seemed to get carried away in excitement of this account. She continued, 'I did well to help pin them down, holding one of their neck so tightly that onlookers yelled at us, "Chinese murderess!" and rushed to save their poor necks from our hands. We noticed with disbelief after we were separated from them that they became more tranquil and retreated, uttering curses upon us.

'Before long, we were perceived with scorn and hatred.

Our freedom in the ghetto became slightly restricted. Most everyone, afraid of being ejected, started to single us out and found fault with almost anything we did. We realized there was a cold sanction against us.

'We learned later that the men happened to be in close liaison with some corrupt police forces. When a ghetto mate alerted us of this, we sneaked out the next morning.

'As Min Lieu and I were in such a hurry to get over to another ghetto, we didn't notice an approaching police car. All we noticed was what looked like another migrant making his own way. We turned quickly, and to our surprise, the police car was almost at a halt near us. Lieu was long gone yelling at the top of his voice, "Run, Lucy, run!"

'I took a quick glance around me. The only option was to risk ascending a fenced wall on my right. As I climbed, onlookers applaud in disbelief. I remained amazed at my own effort for a long time afterwards.

'Had it not been out of terror, I would never have been able to climb to such a height. I commended myself to Buddha and retreated quickly, in hot pursuit of my Lieu to Shanghai ghetto, miles away from the other one.

'Later that evening, others returned to tell their day's ordeal.

We heard an amazing variety of stories about how each had survived the day.'

Lucy smiled and tapped *Ali's* left shoulder. 'Anyway, never mind, you guys will be fine.'

'But, please excuse me,' *Ben* insisted, wanting to know more. 'You never said what happened to your leg.'

Lucy shrugged and shook her head calmly back and forth.

Then she asked, 'Do you really have the heart to hear this?'

Ali was speechless, but *Ben* politely insisted, 'Oh please,

Lucy.'

Twelve

'Life in the ghetto was still bubbling, and no one was ready to give financial help to anyone else,' Lucy began. 'Lieu had a surprised the next morning. A young man came to the ghetto to see a friend. On seeing Lieu, he said, "Hi! It seems I know you.'

'"Oh, yes!" Lieu cried without the least hesitation.

'The man was an old friend from back home in Fujuan. He and Lieu hastily exchanged greetings, and he asked us to come with him to his place of abode. He didn't tell us the condition of the place.

'We at long last arrived at the place. It was a factory yard, and the product was floor tiles. The accommodations were free but with only one rule. The condition here was that we had to use the wooden pallets meant for the tiles as our mattress, and we were to stay away from the factory premises during the day to avoid begin seen by the working staff. We had to wake up early, rearrange the pallets exactly as they were, and disappear, no matter the conditions of our health or the weather.

'And we could only return at dusk. We had to keep to this schedule, to make it safer for the few migrant workers among the lot who had to risk their jobs in sympathy to give us such assistance. The benefit of having free lodging and the added luxury of being able to stay the whole weekend, usually after Fridays when no workers were expected was worth the sacrifice.

'From this new abode, my husband came into contact with other foreigners who were living and working in the area.

Lieu did his best to search for a job, and at long last, he found one.

'The night before his first day, he couldn't sleep. He sat up waiting for daylight, when he was to be introduced to the manager of a nearby company. He did his best to keep his attire clean, and soon, he was standing before the director.

'"What is your name?" the director asked.

'"Lieu, Lieu Ming," he answered.

'"Can I have a look at your passport?" the director demanded.

'Lieu obliged, knowing very well that the passport was forged. He felt his heartbeat leap, nearly choking his breath as the director scanned his passport. The few seconds that passed seemed like hours for Lieu.

'"Okay!" the director said, breaking the silence. 'You may come tomorrow morning to commence your duty."

'The tension diffused, and Lieu's heartbeat quickly returned to normal.

'The next day, he commenced the job as promised. As his wife, I was allowed to join him in the accommodations provided. We had the privilege of sleeping on a mattress, for the first time in months.

'The unfortunate thing for Lieu was that his job had no starting or ending time. He was more or less used for any kind of job, ranging from making coffee to serving clients to helping a welder to keeping stock, and he also served as night watchman.

'For all this, he was promised a meagre salary, which he didn't receive for two months. In no time, Lieu was fed up with the job, but he couldn't leave immediately, as jobs were very limited. He was also bound to stay on so that he could collect his unpaid salary before vacating the job. We were shocked to find ourselves waiting for this money, which finally came at the end of the third month.'

'No way!' *Ben* said, jerking her neck forward. 'That was a very bad experience, wasn't it Ali?'

'It was,' *Ali* agreed. 'But at least you were paid, right?' she added.

Lucy leaned back, raising her feet in the air as an exclamation.

'Yes we did get it, and getting food wasn't too difficult either.

He did make sure we had 20 per cent of our wages every month to enable us to eat, as Lieu would point out, and he was generous because he paid us every penny in the end.'

She paused for a while and added in a low tone, 'Ah, God will surely bless that man.'

'I guess the director might have been a good man,' *Ali* reflected, 'because some people simply get the police to arrest the migrants after their salaries have accumulated.'

'Oh poor souls. I feared that was where your story was going,' *Ben* added.

'What happened next?' *Ali* enquired.

Lucy seemed to get lost when she was narrating her story.

'Er—oh yes.' She wailed and then went on. 'Then one cold winter morning, Lieu was busily sweeping the yard. A Toyota Land Cruiser, which looked slightly yellow, emerged through the gate and screeched to a halt. Lieu turned to look without any alarm and then went back to sweeping.

'I overheard a shout from one of the young men in the front seat. "Hey," he called. As I was peeping through our room window louvers, Lieu turned towards the man, thinking it might be a customer.

'The man quickly threw a question at my husband. "Where do you come from?"

'Familiar with the way some of the customers asked questions to appease their curiosity, Lieu was reluctant and failed to reply. Just when Lieu turned to continue sweeping, the man jumped hastily from the car. He wore camouflage pants and military boots and wielded an AK-47. He looked not very tall but was stoutly built, and the one behind the steering wheel looked much bigger when he came down.

My heart leapt, and so did Lieu's, as I could tell from my hiding place. His face suddenly looked purple and pale.

'Seized with horror, I quietly put our room light out and discreetly locked the door. The second man quickly approached the door. I dashed and slid under the bed. He tried the door and uttered something in Arabic. He repeated the same word again. *He has seen me*, I thought. I was about to come out of my hiding place, when he walked away. I got up and peeped through the window again.

'The man wielding the gun smacked Lieu's cheek with the back of his hand, ordering him to get into the car, which I could now see was fully loaded with similarly young illegal aliens. Lieu's fellow workers, Egyptians and Palestinians, who were free to live and work in Shuebha, stood watching, speechless. They dared not say anything.

'Lieu later told me that at first he couldn't believe what was happening. He thought he was hallucinating.

'They shortly found Willie, a co-worker who was standing in a perplexed state of horror as he watched the wildness of the policemen, whose number had increased to ten and who were now violently kicking every locked door in searched of more illegal aliens. Then came a sudden pinch of the whip on his back as one of the men ordered him to run in front of them. He doubled his pace to avoid further punishment.

'From my hiding place, I perceived more cars and long buses approaching the gate. As they advanced closer, I saw scores of policemen fully armed standing in the buses and shouting instructions. "Come on! Get on board."

'Lieu was forced to embark and was surprised to see Willie among the dozens of illegal foreign nationals. Willie lowered his eyes in shame. He had maintained that he was born in Arabia, not knowing it was a lie. Willie moved to Arabia seven years ago from Yemen and had managed to acquire fake Arabian passport with the pretext that he was a native.

'"How did this happen to you?" Lieu started to ask.

'Willie became furious and cried, "Stop It! I foresaw this coming and warned you not to open the main gates in the early mornings, but you never listened to me, did you?"

'Lieu, highly discouraged, only gazed calmly at Willie. Without uttering a word, he looked away in disappointment.

'"Now see where we are?" said Willie.

'"This is a special operation; they would have jumped over our gates or walls had they found it locked!" Lieu finally said.

'"Are you sure," Willie asked.

'"Yes!" replied a tall lanky young man, among those who had already been caught at a different location. "They did just that to us!" He paused, and then added, "Willie."

'"How do you know my name?" Willie demanded.

'The man smiled and shook his head. "It doesn't matters anymore. I heard him call your name; that's all. "It wasn't easy," he continued. "I went to the gate when they banged on it, and on seeing them, I retreated without opening it."

'He paused and said, "Look at them. They are highly trained. Some had already jumped into our yard before they banged on the gate."

'"How do you know that?" Willie asked.

'"As soon as I retreated from the door, I was given a hot chase by two policemen within our compounds, firing warning shots. So, Mr Willie, tell me, how did they get in whilst the main gate was still locked?"

'The stories of those on board the bus and the testimony of the tall lanky man, who later asked to be called Musah, confirmed the seriousness attached to the operation. The whole area was flushed out of any illegal aliens, who ranged from most Third World countries. The group included some women accused of prostitution, but the majority were men.

'While those on board continued to talk about the situation in which they found themselves, the convoy left our compound, heading towards the high street. But I still could not move. I was full of fear.

'Suddenly, I heard a gunshot. *What is it?* I cried to myself.

Lieu later told me that, to everyone's surprise, two young men were trying to escape. The warning shot had made them give up. They were caught and both their hands and feet were bound. Willie, Lieu, and all those detained on the bus could not imagine the sort of trouble the attempted escapees had created for themselves.

'In no time at all, the convoy was heading towards the nearest military barracks.

'The reality of the day started to emerge as they were kept on the bus for over two hours. This increased their fears as to where they would be taken. A part of the group feared they would be driven deep into the desert and left there.

'Willie needed to urinate. But when he asked the officer on board, he received two violent slaps. He was forced to stand still and keep his discomfort to himself. Had it not been for the timely intervention of a superior officer who asked all of them to disembark and sit on the earth, he would have sung a bad tune in the bus.

'They were kept in that position for hours, at which point another batch of immigrants was brought in. This time, two young men among the lot were bound together facing each other, with a bottle full of some white liquid in their hands.

'Willie whispered to Lieu, "What have they done?"

"'Guess," Lieu replied. "Look at what they hold in their hands."

'Willie, rather unassumingly, took a closer look at the two men and shook his head in contempt. "Oh my god. Those men are in real trouble," he said.

'Lieu smiled at him and asked, "You've got it now, right?

What do you think could be their possible alleged crime?"

"'They are alcohol dealers," he yelled out of anger.

"'Hey, shush," Lieu cautioned, telling him to keep his voice low.

'Willie calmed down briefly and whispered to Lieu, "I can assure you that brewing alcohol is highly forbidden in Arab countries, and innocent people like us who are indisputably willing to obey rules just to work for some money get into trouble because of these greedy guys' illegal activities. Look at how their poor lips are oozing with blood, depicting some sort of violent torture. I would not be surprised if they even sold other illegal drugs," Willie concluded.

'They were soon reloaded onto the buses and driven off, none of them having idea where they were going. They were driven through a date palm plantation. *Should I jump out of these windows into the dark plantation and escape?* Lieu contemplated. But the thought of possibly being shot by the police guards made such an attempt unappealing.

'The bus finally came to a halt in an enclosed yard; they were forced to form rows so they could be counted and marched in at the exact time for dinner.

'"Taboo!" yelled one of the inmates, who was standing beside the guard.

'"He might be the cell leader," Willie suggested.

'The response to the order was that of unison, each person stopped whatever he or she was doing to queue up in tens.

There was some sort of struggling, which most of the newcomers didn't understand.

'Meanwhile, the two alcohol dealers were separated from the lot.

'Almost immediately, the food pots were emptied. A few, including Willie and Lieu, got nothing to eat except the excess water left behind in buckets.

'"What do we do now?" one of them asked.

'"Let's ask that policeman if he could get us some food,"

Willie replied.

'"Please no!" another person said, trying to stop Willie from asking, as doing so might turn out to be trouble for him.

'Willie stood still for a while and then moved on, standing in front of the policemen. "Please, sir, we did not get any food," he said.

'The uniformed guard looked at Willie for a while without uttering a word. He held his tobacco against his lips and signalled to Willie to move away.

'Without hesitation, Willie turned to leave. When he had taken two steps away from the guard, the guard pounced on him, lashing him with a cable. Willie screamed and took to his heels in shock, moving into the crowded cell. The guard swore at him and retreated to his standing position near the entrance.

'It was a harrowing experience to see inmates violently beaten at the slightest mistake. Lieu couldn't stop thinking about how he was going to get out of this place. He thought of making an escape but withdrew the idea when an inmate told him that two young men were shot and badly wounded in the leg the previous night in their attempt to escape and another two, who had been held, were brought back having been messily whipped.

'The assemblage slogan sounded again, "Taboo!" Lieu was again found wanting. *What does it mean?* he wondered.

He did not remember that the same call had sounded the previous day before dinner was served. He carefully stepped aside and watched the movement of the inmates, as well as that of Willie.

'Everyone lined up in tens. Without further hesitation he also joined. The two suspected alcohol dealers, still tied together, were pulled out.

'Being Lieu's first time to witness such treatment, he was shocked to see these two young men tied with a thick rope and whipped on the bottom of their feet with a thick, hard plastic tube. The wailing and crying was so unbearable that Lieu promised himself never ever to plan an escape.

'The next thing on his mind on his third day of detention, which happened to be the deportation day, was his three months' unpaid salary. Thus, he was highly dispirited. How he wished he could have had this money on him before being deported. He perched miserably in a corner trying to recollect the dreadful adventures that had led him to this place; he had achieved nothing but a humiliating deportation. It was too much for him, to the extent that he shed litres of disappointed tears.

'And then a young soldier—the most feared among the lot—arrived. The whole room quickly fell into silence. Lieu hurriedly wiped the tears away and forced up a smiling face.

Everyone stopped whatever he or she was doing and sat still, wondering who might the recipient of the approaching trouble.

'The soldier gazed upon the migrants in silence. Then he broke the silence, "Who is Lieu?" he demanded.

'*Oh! What have I done?* Lieu asked himself. His heartbeat increased. *Perhaps someone has reported my earlier desire to escape to the guard*, he thought. *But I have committed no wrong.* Then calmly, he responded, "Please, sir, I am Lieu."

'The soldier paused, took a brief look at Lieu, and then said, "Come! Follow me."

'Lieu followed him; trembling with fear and horror, he nearly fell to the floor. The looks on the faces of the inmates revealed the pity they felt for him; everyone knew that whenever anyone was singled out, it meant trouble.

Lieu followed this young man quickly until they had left the compound.

'To his greatest shock and relief, he saw his boss. The man had come and had managed to negotiate his released. Lieu beamed unceasingly when, together with Willie, they at last sat in a Mercedes Benz and were driven away. The camp was soon out of sight.

'Finally my husband joined me and was back at the workplace. Nothing compared to my happiness that day.'

Thirteen

Lucy paused. 'You asked me to tell you what happened to my leg, didn't you?' she asked.

The Almonds nodded. 'Yes, if you can,' Ali said.

'For three months after Lieu's first arrest, we lived without any trouble,' Lucy continued. 'We doubled our efforts to work hard to win more favour. This time, he received three months' salary.

'Soon, news of brutality against immigrants in the city centre reached us, and it sent shivers down Lieu's spine.

His distraction caused him to sustain a bad wound from an electric disc cutter on his right forefinger. He was rushed to the hospital in under a few minutes for stitches and scheduled to return a few days later.

'To avoid any further arrest, we resolved to shop during the twilight hours. And when it was not possible to get what we needed, we managed to sneak into the markets during the very early hours of the day.

'We did our best to store more foods. Frozen chickens and live ones were the cheapest meat we could afford. Having had enough or too much of this meat, we judged it sensible to seek a change for a day at least.

'We opted for fresh fish. Together with two co-workers, Willie and Mass, we took the risk one Friday morning. At that time, the manager of our company was on a business trip in Malta. We hastily got ourselves into the market without any trouble, and hurriedly we got what we needed.

'On our way to catch the taxi home, Willie tried to convince Mass to accompany him to visit some hidden prostitutes.

Willie even pledged to use his money to pay for Mass's visit.

'"Can you guys come with me and wait? I won't take long.

Please," he insisted. "I should be done in twenty minutes.

Then we can go back together."

'But we all strongly opposed his wish; perhaps Lieu and Mass were shy in my presence.

'We collected the fish and vegetables from him as he parted ways from us. "See you guys later at our place of abode," he said as he took a left turn into a narrow alley.

'We turned in the opposite direction and descended a step along the road to catch a taxi. I was so upset with Willie's proposal that I hastily stepped forward, reached out for the front seat of the taxi, and took a seat.

'Upon seating I observed, to my great dread, two police cars—an Audi 80 and a Volvo painted black and white—approaching. One drove to a stop right in front of the taxi, and the other pulled up almost right against the side opposite the one in which I was seated. There was little we could do to escape. I hadn't noticed their approach earlier, and neither had Lieu or Mass, who were both attempting to apologize on behalf of Willie's careless invitation.

'The police officers soon gave us the order. "Kai, come down!" We did, and I knew what was about to happen. I cursed myself for not agreeing to Willie's awkward proposal to visit the prostitutes. I guessed both guys might have thought likewise.

'"What is your name? And where do you come from?" They asked two questions at a time.

'I hadn't even opened my mouth to answer, when one pulled me by the shirt collar to the back of the Volvo. He opened the boot and ordered me to get into it. I turned to look at him in a rather polite way. Using my left hand, I rubbed my hair. "Mudee," I said, "please I beg you." He had smiled at me earlier, but he frowned immediately when I tried to beg.

'He kicked me in the stomach. I winced and bent over as pain spread through my abdomen. He had not an ounce of sympathy. He next used his police boot to kick my protruding back, sending my whole body and head smashing against the opened door. I could see the other three men approaching and that one was about to use the end of his gun to hit me.

'Sensing more violence against me, I quickly jumped into the car boot and coiled in silence. Lieu, who already knew how ruthless the police could be, had uttered no word but had quickly squeezed himself, together with Mass, into the Audi car boot before I was forced into the Volvo boot.

'They violently closed the boot over me. I thought that was the end of us. They kept us in the boots and drove around town, even stopping somewhere for a snack. They didn't bother to check on us. We were soaked in sweat in the dark car boots. When they finally took us out, we looked around to see where we had been brought. Lieu didn't recognize the place. He was convinced that it wasn't the place where he'd been sent after the first arrest. With the exception of the spicy chillies, everything was collected from us.

'"Come on," cried one of the policemen. He ordered us to follow him to be locked up.

'I had barely taken a step when one of them landed an electric wire cable on my back. I raised a loud cry of despair of horror, turned, and threw both my hands up in despair.

Shortly, I lived to regret doing so.

'Dozens of the uniformed army personnel held and pulled me into a big enclosed hall, where I saw to my amazement, dozens upon dozens of foreign nationals held in detention with no apparent reason other than not having legal documents to stay in the country.

'The place, a disused basketball dome, had parallel iron bars separating the seats from the court. The officers pulled me onto the seat, fastened my hands and legs behind me in between the parallel bars, my body against the bars, making it impossible for me to move. The next thing I knew, they had taken out a thick, hard plastic hose. The sight of it quickly brought tears to my eyes; I sobbed in a pathetic manner, hoping to win some form of mercy.

'My tears had an impact on one of them, a soft-spoken young man who I presumed to be in his late thirties.

Two men stood up with the whips in hand, while the soft-spoken man gestured to the fourth to step aside for some dialogue. The whole detention centre was dead silent.

The increasing voices of the other two guards suggested both were at loggerheads. I could not understand the exact words, but I could tell that one was negotiating for my release. Defenceless as I was, I could only wait and hope.

'One among the three standing behind the two men trying to reach a deal seized the plastic tube and started to hit me on the bottom of my foot.

'I wailed and cried out for help, which never came. The soft-spoken guard, who seemed likely to be attempting an act of kindness, threw both hands into the air in desperation and walked off. I could hardly count the number of strokes I received, but I guessed it was close to thirty.

'After awhile, they had trouble stopping my uproars, so they paused. Though in pain, I was inwardly glad that it was over. I watched with utmost despair when they returned to gag me with a cloth to muffle my cries. Somewhere along, I lost track of what was going on, and I passed out.

'For the first two few days in the centre, I could not walk.

Neither could I stand on both feet, due to the acute pain.

Bound with the duty to stand like everyone else for roll call, as well as during the struggle for food, I managed to do these things by holding onto Lieu and thanks to the kindness of those willing to help.

'"Taboo" was the call for all to stop whatever he or she was occupied with and line up in tens; if you were caught being slow to respond, you'd incur ten lashes on the bottom of the foot.

'The food we received was, by no means, nutritious. Porridge without milk or sugar was served as breakfast. Dinner was always rice cooked in a tomato sauce.

'Bathing was excluded from our rights. The toilet facilities, which could not contain such population, were soon in disuse; piles of defecate soon found their way out of the disused restrooms, making the smells in the room unbearable.

'Smoking became the only temporary remedy, as some of the guards traded in tobacco. I had long hated the slightest smell of tobacco, but loved it fervently during this time.

Though I resisted the temptation to smoke, we could not help sitting very close to anyone smoking just to escape the sickening stench in that enclosure.

'We slept on the bare open floor. The untidy nature of the place boosted a leech population. My body soon fell under total control of the parasites. At night, scores of inmates lay awake with their shirts and shorts taken off as these tiny nocturnal bloodsucking creatures hunted wildly. And I, being a woman among the mostly male population in the detention centre, found it even harder to go topless.

'The lights were kept on all the time; we noted day from night only through a small opening far above that was covered in barbed wire.

'Lieu and I spent nine days in this hell without any hope of being deported, let alone let free. The latter was not a possibility, but we kept hoping for the unthinkable to happen.

'"Taboo! Taboo!" came the call one day. Then five armed guards came rushing in. We all quickly lined up in tens and were ordered to hold hands.

'We were ushered outside for the first time in a week—the first time in months for others.

'I could hardly walk. Lieu's wounded finger was getting bad. He drew the attention of one policeman and pointed to his wound, saying that it needed to be redressed and, if possible, the stitches needed taken out.

'Lieu was brushed aside. "Look," the man said, "get away!

And don't dare talk about your dirty hands again. Do you understand?"

'"Yes, sir!" Lieu answered. He quickly took leave of the officer. I felt sharper pains in my feet than usual.

'As my fears and worries that I might not be able to walk properly again increased, my husband, who had been scheduled to return and have his stitches removed on the day we were arrested also found himself in pain. We were locked up, along with nearly two hundred others, without any prospect of hope.

'One day, an idea struck Mass with lightning force, and he was soon on his feet. "Let's explore the abandoned toilets," he told Lieu. "There might be some loophole to escape from."

'Leaving me behind to keep watch, they soon acted on Mass's plan.

'The toilets were no longer in use, so the floors near the toilets were covered with excreta. Mass and Lieu managed to tiptoe in the mess, exploring all the rooms, which were very dark. After a careful search, Mass spotted an opening at the very top of the room, about twenty feet high. This meant they would need something like a ladder, which would be impossible to get.

'"What do we do now?" Lieu asked.

'Then they heard the cry of, "Taboo! Taboo!"

'Hastily, we sneaked out making gestures to indicate we had been using the toilets. In no time, we rejoined the rest for the count.

'The cause of this gathering was to discipline an inmate who was caught in an attempt to escape—by which means, I had no idea. The guards dished out a severe beating. His wailing and cries for forgiveness demoralized us, and we abandoned our efforts and hopes of escapes that night.

'The next morning, Lieu asked, "You know that, if we are caught, that is how we'll be treated, right?"

'"Yes, of course!" cried Mass. "But what do you think will happen if we just stay here? Look, let's forgets about negative thoughts and just try our luck!" he concluded.

'So we waited patiently that evening until the usual struggle and hullabaloo associated with our late-night supper started. We seized the opportunity and sneaked undetected to the place Mass and Lieu had found the previous day.

We carefully searched the dark room, trying to determine how we could ascend. In the course of this search, Mass planned our escape. "Yes!" he whispered. "We can use this method!"

'"Which method?" I asked.

'"Please, give me one of your hands," he said.

'I hastily handed over my left hand, and to my surprise, he led it onto a vertical metallic water pipe firmly pinned against the wall. "Ah!" I cried in ecstasy. "Look, it goes right up to the top!"

'Overwhelmed with joy, we got set to go.

'Lieu was the first to try it. He easily succumbed to the acute pain he felt from his wounded finger. He hastily moved from that place to a slightly lighter spot and looked at the bandage stained in fresh blood.

'Next, Mass quickly ascended. Reaching the top, he squeezed his body through the opening and disappeared.

I was stunned. "Look! He is gone!" I cried out softly to my husband. "Can you try again, Lieu?" I encouraged him.

'"Go on if you can; save yourself. Don't worry about me," he replied.

'I took consolation and hope from his words and climbed.

I called to Lieu for the last time to come on then jumped out and took to my heels into the nearby plantation, where Mass was waiting.

'*They have gone, leaving me alone! Oh God!* thought Lieu, feeling devastated. He looked up again at this potentially brilliant chance for freedom. But his wound was an obstacle.

No! he said to himself. *I have to turn deaf ears to the pains from this wound and take this chance.*

'Weighing the merits of a second attempt against it flaws, he was convinced that it could be, indeed, worth trying. He grabbed the pipe with both hands and started to ascend.

This time, highly determined not to give up, he exchanged the acute pain for shrill cries. In truth, by the time he got to the top, he was in tears.

'Squeezing his body through the opening, he jumped off and landed quite well on both feet. Taking a look around, he saw Mass and I forging ahead through the plantation.

He followed in full gallop without hesitation.

'When we had covered about two miles, we heard a rattling behind us, as if someone was giving us chase. We slowed to pay close attention to the noise. We perceived that the rattling was getting closer! This paved the way for another endless marathon.

'The notion that the policemen might be behind us made us run all the more. And despite the acute pain in my leg and my abdomen, partly a result of not having eaten for the whole day, I did not succumb—not until what we presumed to be a ferocious enemy cried out dejectedly, "Ah!

Please stop and let's have some rest!"

'We stopped and realized that the person following us was an inmate who had been able to detect our move and capitalized on it.'

Lucy lowered her gaze. Her eyes moistened with tears. She paused for a brief second and then concluded, 'We managed to escape, but I have never walked properly since.'

Fourteen

Lucy's story made the sister's mood heavy.

However, the Almonds' hope was somewhat revived when they heard the success story of another group of immigrants who had made it, without apprehension, to the big city.

This compelled them to join another group preparing to take off. By now, two-thirds of their savings had gone to frantic efforts to move ahead.

During all their attempts, they had been full of much hope of succeeding, but with this particular trip, they were more nervous than hopeful. *Ali* thought, with resignation, as she looked around the migrants that perhaps none of them displayed the least amount of hope because of the departure time and the greater number of immigrants involved. The trip began in the hot sunshine in a truck that looked very old and hissed loudly from every angle. All were filled with anxiety as the truck accelerated.

To their astonishment, the truck escaped the first and most cruel police barrier unnoticed. The convoy forged ahead gradually until darkness had taken over the daylight.

They had advanced thirty miles in the dark when the truck screeched to a halt. The joyous mood of the migrants was overtaken by a dreadful silence when scores of military men climbed into the truck and stood over them.

Obeying their orders to disembark, the migrants were soon ordered to stand in line. When the group had met the soldiers' demand, two of the soldiers, who looked much more muscular and stronger than the others, advanced towards them. Ben was petrified at their size.

Each migrant was physically assaulted, as badly as they had been during earlier encounters with the military men.

Adding insult to injury, each migrant was expected to beam a smile immediately after being slapped on the cheek and, in turn, ordered to get on board. One by one, each migrant was whacked on the ear, until only the last three remained.

Directly in front of the Almonds was a young man. He received a hard whack on his left ear and screamed loudly.

Ben's heartbeat raced. *This might be my heaviest beating yet*, she thought nervously, her jaws clenched tightly shut as she waited her turn.

The failure of the young man to smile infuriated the soldiers.

They pounced on him, kicking and punching him until he bled profusely.

After making certain they had thoroughly bullied the unsmiling young man, the soldiers turned to the Almonds, the last two migrants remaining on the ground. *Ben* braced, but the soldiers merely gestured for the sisters to join the rest in the truck. This the Almonds did with joy.

Meanwhile, the driver is engaged in a lengthy conversation with the head soldier little distance away from light. The soldier then shrugged and paced around, both hands in pocket. He moved back towards the driver and there was a swift exchange of hands. The soldier smile and shook the driver's hand. It became obvious that money or some other valuable consideration has been given or promised thus corrupting the behavior of the soldiers.

Despite the bullying, the truck was filled with joy, as its occupants had been informed that there would be no any further trouble ahead. And as the truck made its way to the main metropolis, they engaged in hearty conversation.

The truck came to a final halt in a farmyard at midnight.

The driver, expecting the migrants to jump off and stretched their tired bodies, became alarmed when he waited for five minutes and no migrants emerged.

Creek. The driver's front door hissed loudly as he made his way out to ascertain what was amiss. He looked quite old, tired, and feeble but managed to climb into the 1960 Russian-built KAMAZ dump truck.

For a few seconds, he looked at the migrants. None made a move, and the man was lost in thought. The driver soon regained his senses. He was surprised to see that all the migrants were fast asleep. He banged on the hard metallic body of the truck.

The weary group jumped off the truck and stretched their tired bodies.

While each migrant took a seat and began to appease the call of hunger, the Almonds judged it sensible to move in and make some acquaintances. But extricating themselves from among the other migrants within the hedges around the farm wasn't quite easy.

On approaching the road, *Ali* made an important decision.

The choice was that they decided to have a brief nap under some nearby hedges due to exhaustion. A car screeched to a halt. 'How did you get here?' a voice enquired.

Ali and Ben looked up and saw a young man dressed in a modern pink embroidered silk kurta that fell to his ankles. His face looked familiar to them, but they couldn't immediately recollect from where.

Ali, in the end, exclaimed, 'Oh hi. It's you! We just came with a truck, which is long gone.'. Harris Hammond, the young man who had led them to the Malanga ghetto in Al Wajh 'Well, do you want to get in?' Harris asked. 'Come on—'

'No,' Ben snapped at Ali, who was moving towards the car.

'Have you considered the risk?'

'Hurry, Ben. Don't you remember him? He saved us from the curfew.'

Ben turned away, unwilling to compromise, to the discomfort of the young man.

Probably because he was a Somali native like them, Harris was the first to address the sisters as females in the two years since they had embarked on their quest to reach the United Kingdom.

This he did to the great distaste of *Ben* in particular. She burst out in anger, yelling at the young man in their native language. 'How on earth do you know we are women?' she demanded.

'Stop it, *Ben,' Ali* interrupted.

'Leave me alone,' *Ben* snapped back. 'Think about it. How could he recognize us in this dark and stop by if he wasn't spying on us or something?' She paused and glared at Harris.

'Are you stalking us? What do you want from us? You son of a bitch; get lost!'

Ali stood still, shocked at her sister's behaviour. At last, she raised her voice. 'Calm down, *Ben.'*

The scene became unbearable for the young man. He quietly sat back in his white Cadillac and drove off in embarrassment.

From there, the sisters did not speak to each other for almost an hour, but they did manage to use a piece of a map that Lucy had given them to locate a cheap migrant ghetto in Diriyah, about 25 kilometres away from the capital.

At 6.09 a.m., they had arrived at the door, but they were too terrified to knock.

When you get there, remember to ask for Lee Yung. Just mention my name, Lucy Tina, and he will take care of you. He should be able to. They both remembered Lucy's wards.

Ben was now fifteen years old, and the hardships of their journeys had somehow transformed her from a quiet, shy, and timid girl to nothing less than a tough boy. She took a deep breath and banged on the door.

A female voice responded instantly. With the door slightly ajar, the woman beckoned. 'Please come in,' she said.

They stepped in, and the door was quickly shut.

They had very little difficulty in locating Lee Ming Yung.

He was a much more heavily built man than was normal for men of the Far East. He looked to be in his late fifties and had heavy, slightly reddish cheekbones.

'Did you say Lucy Tina?' he asked as *Ali* handed over a concealed note from Lucy to him.

This he took some steps away and read silently; in the end, he smiled and said, 'All right; let me show you your room.'

The sisters were given a small room with a mattress for the first time in their life. 'I will take you around the city later today, probably after breakfast and the next day, I will take you to your employer,' Lee Yung told them.

Ben quickly looked at *Ali*. Each recognized the concealed joy within her sister, but both managed not to look too excited. 'Thank you, Mr Lee,' they responded at the same time.

'Please, come out for breakfast,' a voice said with a tap on their door. They girls hesitated not at all to join Mr and Mrs Lee at their table, as the call of hunger had grown very strong.

It was a typical traditional Arabian breakfast. They sat at a long table, Mr and Mrs Lee at the far end and the Almonds together across from each other at the other end. The table was filled with a variety of offerings; a small coffee kettle and a bowl of dates sat at one side. The main course was served, along with a variety of small plates and bowls of olives. Also present on the table were two types of cheese, honey, jams, scrambled eggs, and fresh hot bread, shaped in large flat circles. On the left hand corner next to Mr Lee stood a boiling kettle filled with dried tea leaves on a small cylindrical glass stove. He took the kettle and served each of the young women in a small slender glass filled to the brim but loaded heavily with sugar, to the dislike of Ali.

'So how was your journey?' Mrs Lee asked, speaking for the first time.

'Fine,' Ali replied.

'Hell no, it wasn't fine,' Ben snapped, looking scornfully at her sister. 'The trip was terrible. We were beaten, and we've had to sacrifice a lot to get here,' she concluded.

The elder sister said nothing more but quietly ate her breakfast.

No one spoke for the next five to ten minutes.

Right at the end of the meal, when they were clearing the breakfast table, Mrs Lee said, 'Have you ever heard of the Golden Ventures?'

'Golden Ventures? No,' the girls answered.

'Well, I and my husband, Lee, were one of them.'

'One of them? Please, what do you mean by that?' *Ben* asked.

'In 1993, we were among about 300 Chinese immigrants who boarded a ship to the United States. The aged ship ran aground off New York City, and the water was ragged.

We were asked to swim to escape or would be arrested and deported. Some braved it, but—' she stammered a bit. 'I think nine or ten people died in that tragedy.'

'Really?' *Ali* lamented. 'Why are you in Arabia instead of the United States?

'Our asylum request was turned down, and we were deported. We tried another move but failed again. In the end, we made it to Arabia, and it's not bad here at all. We did not plan to be here, but we took our opportunity, and now we are happy. Aren't we, Lee?'

Mr Lee nodded with a smile and a raised fist.

'How long have you been living here then?'

'Seven years in total,' Mrs. Lee told her.

'And how many of those years have you been to China to see your families?' Ben asked.

"Not yet, but we will go very soon.'

'How did you and Lucy get to know each other?'

'Ben,' Ali said gently, patting her sister's shoulder as a sign of disapproval at having asked too much.

'Tina is our only daughter,' replied Mrs Lee without hesitation Ben nodded in silence and said no more; neither did her sister.

A few minutes later, the Almonds were driven by Mr Lee in a Skoda car across Riyadh Township. They marveled at the commercial skyscrapers located in the business district.

'Ah,' exclaimed *Ben* as she tipped her head backwards, trying to catch a glimpse of the very tip of a particular building.

'That is too tall!'

'That,' Mr Lee responded, "is Al Faisaliyah Center. After the Kingdom Centre, it is the second tallest building in Saudi Arabia.'

They pulled over. Ali and Mr Lee alighted and leaned on the car, but *Ben* remained in the back seat of the car with the windows lowered.

'Do you know how tall it is?' Ali asked, a bit curious.

"The Al Faisaliyah Center is about 267 meters high and consists of forty-four floors.'

'And what is below it, please?'

'Immediately below it is an outside viewing deck; at ground level, there is a shopping centre that offers all the major world brands.'

The two sisters, satisfied with Mr Lee's answers, nodded in excitement when he added, 'Tomorrow morning, you should be prepared to meet your employer in that building.'

It felt like a perfect day.

Suddenly a coach swayed out from the opposing lane of traffic and flew towards them.

'Hey! Get out!' yelled Mr Lee, rushing to pull Ben from the car.

Chaos ensued, and what followed next happened too quickly for the girls to keep an eye on the approaching danger. Pedestrians fled in all directions.

The coach crashed into Mr Lee's car, sending the driver side door flying off its hinges. The Almonds managed to get out unscathed, but were alarmed to see Mr Lee lying on the ground, with one arm ripped off.

The girls moved toward the bleeding Lee to comfort him.

'Leave this place now,' he shrieked. 'The police will be coming, and they will ask for your visas. Go now! Go!'

Agitated, the Almonds hurried and disappeared out of sight. They managed to walk as quickly as their legs would carry them. They wandered about desperately and, finally, located an alley route back to Mr Lee's house.

They passed through the back of the mosque and came to a small opening leading to the house but were horrified at what they saw. They discovered that the house of the Lee's had been incinerated. Scores of fire service and ambulance crew members, along with a handful of police officers, milled around the burnt building. A place the sisters had left happily an hour ago had suddenly become an unfriendly sight *Ali's* knees gave way, and she slumped to the ground, rigidly trying to hold back her tears.

'Get up. Let's move away from here,' *Ben* yelled. 'We might be approached soon, and that would bring a lot of discomfort for us. You know that, right?'

'But where are we going from here,' *Ali* asked hopelessly, looking up at *Ben*.

'Remember that Lucy Tina told us if we could not locate Mr Lee, there would be another agent at the other end of the park house?'

As Ben spoke, they took another look at the incinerated house and noticed two policemen watching them. 'Why are they looking at us?' Ali enquired in a whisper The sisters looked around themselves to ascertain whether the policemen were looking at something else, but they realized there was nothing else to watch apart from them.

'They will soon be coming here!' Ali noted and leapt to her feet. 'Let's move now.'

The girls disappeared swiftly, in search of their last hope of finding an immigrant agent. For another seven miles, they strictly followed the map that Lucy had drawn for them. When they arrived at their destination, they encountered nothing but a newly constructed dam; there was no trace of any house.

From this place, they scarcely knew where to turn. Ali and Ben found themselves in a perplexing state of indecision!

Short of ideas as to what to do next, they turned left towards the eastern part of the city.

Whilst walking through a small park, *Ali* grabbed her sister, took a step or two backward, and looked on in amusement.

'Ha,' she proclaimed, 'it's Harris Hammond.' She watched the Somalian *Ben* had ridiculed a day earlier.

They watched as Harris argued with a fellow driver, speaking in Arabic. He yelled at the driver as he turned his car and headed towards them on a narrow side street. On seeing the girls, he screeched to a halt and offered them a ride, telling them to board quickly, which they did without hesitation.

Ben, who had raged at Harris the other night, was too embarrassed to look him in the eye.

'So what are you guys doing?' Harris asked.

'We just got stranded again,' *Ali* confessed. 'And, um—we need some help.'

'But I thought your sister said you were fine?' he asked.

'Please never mind; she was just too stressed out last night,'

Ali replied.

'Um—I'm sorry for the other day. I think I yelled too much,'

Ben apologized.

'No, no bad feelings,' Harris replied. 'I know you did the right thing. You don't know me, and your protectiveness is a sign of love for your sister. It's good to protect each other from strangers.'

'Yes, but please forgive me. I think I shouted too much. Are you sure you don't hate me?' Ben asked.

'Not in the least. People shout when they love each other and are trying to protect them. I admire the love you girls have for each other,' he concluded.

'So, what do you do? I mean, what is your job in this country?' Ben added.

'Well, um, I am a diplomat at the British embassy.'

Oh my god, what a perfect coincidence, Ali thought, but she felt too weird to disclose her thoughts.

'We have been hoping to get to the United Kingdom for ages. Maybe you could help,' Ben blurted out, unable to restrain herself.

'Why do you want to go to England?' Harris asked.

'We just like it,' *Ben* answered sharply.

'Well, um—I know of someone looking for some factory help if you want it?'

'Yes! We would like it,' answered the sisters in harmony.

Fifteen

AL-SHADA food processing company was situated seven kilometres north of Riyadh; the factory was well enclosed and had sleeping dorms for migrants but small in production capacity.

The total working staff of four men was made up of a Palestinian, Mallad Bensallah—he was the supervisor and occupied a whole room alone—two Egyptians, Mr Hassam Kamel and Labara Said; and a soft-spoken Russian, Dimitri Yori. The three shared a room.

The Almonds, together with another newly recruited Palestinian migrant, Akram, were told to wait at the reception with their backpacks.

The manager called Mr Bensallah, the foreman, to the office. 'Bensallah,' said the manager, 'these three men are our new staff. Can you take them to see where they will sleep?'

Mr Bensallah nodded. 'Please come with me,' he said, as he descended the steps out of the manager's office.

'Hang on for a moment,' he said as he moved back towards the office. 'Boss,' he said, leaning into the office, 'I cannot keep those two younger men in my room. You know that I keep valuable things like the designing plans and stuff in there.'

'Yes I know, but what would they use those things for? They are only here to work,' the manager assured him calmly.

Mr Bensallah walked towards the new staff; he stopped and scratched his head, trying to think of what to do next. He walked towards the young Palestinian man; held him by the hand, beaming with a smile; and led him to his room.

'You will share this room with me, but not those two. No, I cannot trust them.'

The Almonds could not understand exactly what Bensallah said, but they could clearly see from his body language that he was against sharing the room with them.

The Almond's suspicions were soon confirmed when Bensallah came out and told them, 'I cannot allow you two to share this room with me, so come over here.' He led them to the room of the Egyptians and the Russians. Hassam was not so particular about who shared the room with them, but he was concerned about the number.

'Bensallah, look, we are three in here. Why add two more?

Why not your room? After all, your room is bigger, and you are the only one. The boss said we should share three to a room.'

Bensallah made no further comment. He retreated, only to return with two mattresses, which he threw at the Almonds before going back to continue his work. This eventually led the manager to convert a disused container into a dormitory for the Almonds. For the disguised girls, it was a perfect relief to be in a room by themselves.

For Ali's first day, she worked at the metal printing machine. A fellow migrant from Peru led her to the machine for an initial demonstration. 'This red button is to stop the machine, the green is to operate it, and any time you see the yellow light blipping, it means there is no material in stock.'

Ali nodded in a happy high tone, 'Yes, sir.'

Next, the Peruvian took a metal plate, placed it under the printer, and said, 'Each time, make sure you don't delay in picking out the printed metal.'

He hastened to execute the first sample. The mechanical sound muffled his shrill cry. Blood gushed from the machine, and the Peruvian staggered backwards, holding his arm high above his head in the air. To Ali's despair, she saw that the Peruvian had lost all five fingers.

Both sisters became terrified and decided not to take the job. They wept at the thought of the poor Peruvian. The next morning the Almond's swollen eyes revealed to the manager and their co-workers that all was not well with the two new recruits. *Ali* couldn't hold back her tears as she narrated the episode to the manager, who was just returning from a business trip in the city.

He encouraged them to take up the job and said all will be fine. He even pledged to help by getting the very latest machines. He concluded by saying, 'Let's put our whole trust in Allah, and we will be safe.'

A ray of hope swept through *Ben's* body at the sound of these positive words, and she warmed towards the job. She also managed to talk her sister into regaining her composure.

And *Ali* pulled out a bit from her depression with the added news that the Peruvian was said to be responding well at the hospital.

Notwithstanding that, every single thought of *Ali's* choked her with despair that never seemed to quite go away.

For three days, there was no prospect of hope as *Ali's* first day at work still haunted her.

She tried to throw in the towel exactly one week after the incident. She walked to the manager's office one morning and said, 'Good morning, sir!'

'Good morning,' he replied and added, 'How are you?'

'I'm fine, thank you,' she said. 'But I want to go home as I very much need to regain my balance.'

'Oh! Why?' he asked in a bit of shock. He endeavoured by all means at his disposal to comfort Ali and to encourage her to stay on. But she maintained her stance until Mr Hammond arrived.

'Can I have a word with you in private?' he asked.

She nodded and followed.

'Look,' he said gently. 'I know what happened looked scary, but these things happen rarely, and if you decline this job, where else will you go?'

Hammond's words undoubtedly sank into her mind. She agreed to keep the job, but she and Ben promised themselves to be very wary.

*   *   *

For nearly three months, both sisters worked for Mr Abdulgadir as factory hands without any incident. Shelter was freely provided, but each time they demanded their wages, he kept promising, 'Don't worry. I am keeping it for you until you decide to leave the country.'

On one occasion at the end of the eleventh month, *Ben* made a bold effort and demanded to keep her own salary.

'I am Muslim,' Abdulgadir stressed. 'I fear Allah and can never take your blood money, so don't worry. I will pay you as soon as you decide to leave.'

After unrelenting attempts, they were paid, and the tradition of keeping migrants' cash became a thing of the past in the company.

Mr Harris Hammond visited the Almonds, but each time the encounters were brief. On one occasion, *Ben* confided in her sister about Mr Hammond's advances. *Ali* warned, 'Never, okay? No more mistakes, right? Just ignore him.'

Sixteen

For two years, the Almonds worked peacefully at AL-SHADA Company. Having become used to behaving like men, so did their physical endurance increase. Very often, news of an immigration arrest reached them, and such news was no longer frightening.

At noon on 13 November, barely two weeks after the Muslim Eid, Akram, one of their Jordanian co-workers, marched into the manager's office and narrated a pathetic story. 'I am utterly despondent, boss.' He paused, looked into the manager's eyes, and burst into tears. 'My mom,' he murmured. 'I just heard the news—just two days ago, I spoke to my mom, and she complained of an itchy, burning sensation in her eyes. Today, she is totally blind in both eyes. What am I going to do now?' He moaned. 'I have to go, at the latest, tomorrow to see my mum.'

Upon hearing the sad news, everyone was moved, and all the staff showered Akram with messages of commiseration.

The next morning, Akram bid goodbye to all and promised to come back as soon as the situation with his mother got better.

Barely twelve hours after Akram's departure, a piercing cry came from Bensallah's room. All the co-workers, except for the Almonds—who were very conscious of Bensallah's hatred for them—rushed in to ascertain what was amiss.

From outside, the sisters heard the man's wailing increase as some of their co-workers went in.

'Let's check and see what is amiss. He might have lost a loved one,' *Ali* suggested.

'Look, this man hates us, okay? Just leave him alone,' *Ben* replied sharply.

The girls watched as Bensallah dashed out into the open and ran towards the manager's office. The manager's door was locked. In loss of hope, he dashed back into the open compound of the factory and threw himself onto the ground, shedding tears uncontrollably.

'Well, well, well,' said *Ben*. 'There might be something definitely wrong.'

The Almonds both felt sympathy for the distraught man and walked towards him. 'What is the problem?' *Ben* inquired.

He pointed at his door and said, 'Akram, Akram.' No words followed as he resumed his sobs.

'I fear the worst might have happened to Akram,' Ben said.

But how? He was supposed to have left twelve hours earlier?

Ben thought as she rushed into the room with Ali, both girls' hearts thumping in anticipation of a horrific sight.

'He might be dead,' Ali whispered to herself sadly.

On entering the room, they saw the whole room in total disorder. Bensallah's sleeping mattress was tossed over, and clothing, shoes, and papers were strewn all over. *What is this?* the Almonds wondered, confused that no one was in the room.

The head and tail of the mystery soon unfolded. Akram had bolted with Mr Bensallah's entire six years of savings.

Not keeping savings in a bank was a standard practice among illegal immigrants for obvious reasons—lack of documentations foremost among them. The vast majority of illegals, including the Almonds, devised their own means of saving their hard-earned currency.

Bensallah had chosen to hide his earnings beneath his sleeping mattress. This he did by cutting through the side of his mattress and filling it with his converted dollar bills.

He made sure the opening was glued back well and pushed closely against the wall at all times. Almost always, he made sure no one was around before he visited his safe.

But for reasons unknown to all, Akram had kept an eye on Bensallah always, and when he'd discovered the man's hiding place, he'd smashed everything, stolen the cash, and ran.

Panic ensued among the remaining migrants. Each rushed to revisit his or her concealed safe.

Hassam, the eldest among the Egyptians, was found behind the kitchen digging the earth. *What the hell is he doing?*

Ali and *Ben* wondered.

Hassam dug down about a foot, and to the girls' surprise, he pulled out a small black tightly fastened item. He untied it in a rush. There was a layer and another.

In the end, he stretched out some notes, which Ben thought to be dollar bills. 'Hey look,' the Almonds whispered to each other as they watched on quietly.

With shivering hands, Hassam paused. And then, he started breathing heavily. He pulled off a note and turned it over and over. Then, he pulled out another until he had checked all the notes one by one. He glanced behind himself to make sure no one was watching. Ben and Ali quickly took cover behind the adjacent parallel steel bar.

Satisfied that no one was watching, Hassam took a closer look at the currencies again. Soon what was meant to be secret was no more. He let out a pained yell and rushed out into the open compound, to the amazement of the two spying sisters.

'Ah! Shee! Oh! Allah!' he cried, flicking out the dollar bills in upset.

His Egyptian colleague rushed toward him to ascertain what was amiss. The unpleasant reaction that ensued when he saw Hassam's dollar bills prompted *Ali* and *Ben* to approach them.

To her horror, as *Ali* was handed over a dollar, she saw that the bills had decayed beyond recognition. 'Oh, my God!' she whispered quietly. The majority of the dollar bills, approximately thirty notes, had rotted in the middle. The only way to recognize the bills was their edges, on which the number '100' appeared and the bottom right hand corner, which read 'one hundred dollars' was scripted.

'*Ben,*' *Ali* cried, her voice chill, 'can we check our bills now?

Look at Hassam's bills? All $3,000 have decayed!"

Ben enquired as to their co-worker's method of storage. 'I saw him,' she recalled, 'and he did wrap it in nylon before burying it from the ground, right? Do you think the decay might be due to the heat?'

Ali thought for a moment. 'Um,' she finally said. 'I believe he had been cheated by the currency dealer.'

'What do you mean?' *Ben* enquired.

'I think he was sold a fake currency.'

'Oh my God,' Ben said, her jaw dropping in panic. She felt her heart race. 'Come on. Let's go check our bills.'

Most migrants, very mindful of being deported without recourse—without even the ability to return home to collect their belongings and money—made it a duty to keep their money on them at almost all times. However, a migrant was stabbed quite recently, strip-searched, and robbed by thugs in the eastern province of Riyadh. This had led the very clever migrants to devise other means of saving their cash.

For the Almonds, no safer place could console their souls than to carefully wrap their hard-earned currency into a vinyl bag and stick it deeply inside themselves. Each time they visited the toilet, they make it a point to first defecate on a piece of paper, collect their money, and reinsert after they were finished.

Being in a hurry, Ali and Ben went separate ways. Ben quickly took her sponge dish and made it to the shower room, whist *Ali* made it hastily into the toilet and pushed the door shut. Cramping slightly, she waited silently as the wrapped notes dropped from her anus.

Nearly thirty minutes past before each unlocked the door and walked out with fairly satisfied faces.

'Mine are good, and genuine. What about yours?' *Ali* asked her sister.

'I think my notes are all right too!' *Ben* answered. 'But how do you know—I mean how can you tell—that they are genuine?' *Ben* enquired.

'You can tell by raising the notes to the light and looking for what looks like particles of human hair in the bill.'

'That's all?' *Ben* asked.

'No,' *Ali* assured her. 'I also checked the front of the bills—Benjamin Franklin's image.

'Oh!' she paused and ran back into the bathroom. She moistened a tissue and tried to rub off the image of Benjamin Franklin. No print came off.

She sighed. 'Guess what?' she called to her sister in ecstasy.

'I think all my notes are genuine. Still not quite satisfied, she raised the notes to a source of light and looked for the silver ribbons embedded within the hundreds. Sure that all security features were in place, she was finally satisfied that she had the right notes.

Quickly she wrapped the notes again. She grinned as she tried to insert them into her back passage. Halfway in, the notes fell to the ground.

What is wrong today? she thought. Then she remembered what she was missing. She walked into her room, dipped her finger into a small tub of Vaseline, and casually walked back into the bathroom. A few minutes later she had inserted the bills well and felt no pain.

She reconfirmed the safety of the bills by fingering herself until her hand touched the package. Thus satisfied, she walked out. Soon afterwards, her younger sister also unlocked her hideaway door and stepped out.

Meanwhile, Bensallah was busily lamenting over his lost savings, as was Hassam, whose bills had turned to shredded tissue.

A blaring of a car horn was heard. *Ali* rushed to the gate to enquire; it was the manager, Mudee Salami, in his gold

Mercedes Benz 200. He calmly drove in and came to a halt as *Ali* held the gate opened.

Bensallah rushed up to meet him and, in a hurry, narrated his story. They both stormed the office. Frantic phone calls ensued.

'Ah! *Ben*! Aw!' the manager lamented.

The others were called to the manager's office. 'Lock yourselves up in your rooms,' he told them, 'and make no noise, as the police are coming to investigate the disappearance of Bensallah's money.'

A moment later, they heard the blaring of the police siren at the gate. All took to their heels and hid, hovering quietly.

They were alerted to come out after the police officers had come and gone.

Despite the officers' promise and intensive search to stop Akram from leaving the country, two weeks passed without any sign of the suspect.

At 11.00 a.m. on Thursday, a letter addressed to the manager arrived. His eye lingered on the stamps—a Syrian stamp he clearly saw. *But who do I know in Syria?* he thought. *Ah!* he said to himself, as his heart raced at the thought of Akram.

'Bensallah!' he screamed. '*Taale*! *Taale*. Come!'

Bensallah rushed towards the mudee, who had walked halfway across the compound towards Bensallah's shop.

The men met each other. 'Guess what this letter is!' said the manager. 'Can you open it and let see who it's from?'

Bensallah tore the envelope open agitatedly and got hold of the letter, both hands trembling nervously. He read on silently for a while with a frown. Midway through the letter, he paused, handed over the letter to the recipient, and walked away murmuring in anger.

The content of the letter confirmed that Akram had successfully left the country and was back in Syria. But there was no mention of any stolen cash. What made Bensallah sick to his stomach was that Akram had stated that he would no longer be coming back as he'd promised, since his mom's ill health had deteriorated.

Highly convinced that Akram was the perpetrator, Mr Bensallah was emotionally disturbed and overcome with a sense of guilt. Later that night, he forced himself to reconcile with the Almonds. 'I am very sorry for not giving you the benefit of the doubt,' he told them. 'I should have known not to carry prejudice.'

The sisters accepted his apology in good faith and showed no signs of ill feelings. But *Ben* denounced him inwardly.

Seventeen

'There is a stranger at the gate,' Hassam said, rushing to Ali's side. 'He wants to see you.'

Who knows me here? Ali thought, not only perplexed but scared for obvious reasons. She held her breath and tiptoed towards the locked gate. Pressing against the walls, she peeked through the side hinges to catch a glimpse of the unknown stranger.

It was dark, and she searched the figure closely. 'Ah!' she sighed upon identifying Mr Harris Hammond. *But what on earth is he looking for?* she thought.

She shut her eyes and counted 'one, two, three,' and took a deep breath as she unlocked the gate. 'Hi! What brings you here in such darkness?'

Harris beamed, showing his spotless white teeth in the dark.

'I have a surprise for you guys. I have something coming via Singapore to Japan.'

'Singa—What?' Ali recoiled at the mention of Singapore and restated their ambition. 'We only want to get into the UK, London for that matter. What would I or my sister want to do in Singapore? Ha? Tell me that.'

'Actually, um, can we sit and talk about this?' Hammond requested.

'Well, come in,' she said. They perched themselves on two inclined chairs. The conversation drifted away deep into the night, and at one point, it dawned on them the sort of stigma attached to intimacy among the non-married in Arabia. Worst of all, they could well be seen as a male couple, due to the continued male appearance of the Almonds.

The conversation was adjourned for the night.

*   *   *

A few weeks later, the girls agreed to give the proposed trip to England a try.

Hammond briefly lectured them on the proposed trip to England; they would travel via Singapore to Japan then over to the United Kingdom. When the girls asked why such complexity was involved, he replied, 'I have networks from here to Japan, and it is easier to obtain a British visa from the First World, so in Japan I can easily arrange a visa for both of you to fly to the UK.

'Having said that, you guys might even end up liking Japan. It is a very beautiful country. I have been too many places, but when you get to Tokyo, you'll see at first glance that no place rivals Japan in terms of modernity and cleanliness.'

Ali listened carefully then asked, 'What makes you say that? England too is very beautiful I suppose.'

'Well, um—England is an old city, very old. I mean the houses are old, and the rent will be extremely high for a new migrants like you.'

"No way. You're kidding, right? I can't believe what you are saying. We have long adored images of London—the beautiful big barn, London Bridge, wow!' she yelled in ecstasy.

Hammond invited the two girls to attend a dinner at his home. He came to pick them up on a Thursday night as scheduled, since the next Friday was their day off. He put up a barbeque and grilled some steaks. He supplied soft drinks in abundance to help them enjoy their evening, making the night a delightful one for the Almonds.

They all settled in for the night's sleep. Midway into the night, Ben awoke and found Ali not beside her. After a few minutes, she wandered about the house, wondering where her sister might have gone. After going through the two toilets, she appeared in the kitchen. She stood still as she watched Mr Hammond blowing his nose loudly after snorting something off a plate in the kitchen. He looked up and saw *Ben* staring at him. His facial expression showed that he was concerned but not upset; he showed no sign of anger.

He seems to be enjoying himself, Ben thought, retreating towards the bedroom she was sharing with *Ali*. She bumped into Ali emerging agitatedly from Hammond's room, half naked.

For a few seconds, *Ben* stared at her sister, her gaze penetrating. Anger raced through her mind. They looked at each other briefly. *Ali* knew she has little time to decide what to say. 'Um—I can explain,' she began. 'Please calm down.' *Ali* looked into her sister's eyes, trying to persuade her to listen calmly. 'Please come with me to our room.'

Ben followed without uttering a word.

In the end, she broke her silence, 'How long has this been going on?'

Ali had no choice but to tell her sister the truth. 'About a year,' she said softly.

'A year! You mean twelve full months?' Ben was overwhelmed with anger that she could not control. She took a deep breath to subdue her anger and forced herself to become more tranquil; nothing else mattered. She started to pack her belongings.

'Wait, where are you going?' Ali asked. 'Please don't. I may have offended you, but don't let this taint our dream.'

Ben was deaf to her sister's pleas; her knees gave way as she slumped onto her bed, tears streaming down her cheeks.

She got up and put on her usual blue jeans, hiking boots, and a navy sweater. For nearly four years, neither sister had dressed like a girl in public; male garb had become embedded in their personalities. Ben wiped tears from her cheeks but managed to keep her composure. Seconds later, she scurried towards the door and disappeared from sight.

Ali was on her feet, her hands clutching her chest, he jaw dropped open. She stared at the door where, moments ago, her sister had been standing. *Well that is the end*, she thought dejectedly. She had no idea where her little sister might be heading. But aware of the danger she may have pushed her sister into, she realized she needed to go after *Ben* and try to rebuild her trust.

She had a second thought. *Maybe she'll come back; after all, she has no place to go.* Four hours passed, and *Ali* saw no sign of her sister coming back. Now she realized she had to go out and find her little sister so that she could talk with her.

Ali managed to find *Ben*, and the sister's love for each other survived, but Ali knew that the damage done to *Ben's* ability to trust her was irreparable. *What a shame*, she thought.

'You lied to me, didn't you?' *Ben* finally said, after two awkward hours of silence.

After a moment, Ali responded abruptly. 'I have no preconceived notion of guilt or innocence, but I don't want to be this person—not anymore.' She burst into sobs again.

'It is one mistake after another and another,' Ben cried.

'Do you know what I miss? I miss Mom, Dad, Koshi,

Taba, everyone'—she paused—'including you.'

Ali waited for another awkward five seconds. Then she decided to tell her sister the whole truth. 'Look me in the eye,' she said. 'I did this to protect you, and to protect us, okay? He wanted this in return for our visas. I resisted, but he threatened to have you or blow the lid on us. Are you satisfied now? I did not want to speak to you about this. I love you, Ben!'

The sisters stood and embraced each other.

Ali worked hard to calm her sister's rage towards Harris Hammond. 'Please, just try to pretend you know nothing,' she pleaded.

'Why not call off this trip?' *Ben* suggested.

'Never mind. When we get to England, all these troubles will be long gone.'

For so long, the sisters had found deep satisfaction in focusing on that dream.

The two girls were filled with a mixture of joy and anxiety as they put the finishing touches on their packing in preparation for the next morning's flight. They would leave from the King Khalid International Airport in Riyadh.

They set off at 9.00 a.m. and headed through the free-flowing traffic to the airport, which was located north of Riyadh. *Ali* and Mr Hammond chatted at length, but *Ben* uttered not a single word throughout the entire thirty-minute drive. Her relationship with their agent had become acrimonious following her discovery of what was going on between him and her sister.

In the end, *Ali* turned to her sister and asked, 'How are you feeling?'

Ben responded without hesitation with another question.

'You really ready for this?'

'Yeah,' Ali said. 'We've made some wrong choices before, but now we have found the correct one.'

They alighted and pulled their small suitcases through the departure hall of terminal C—the terminal used for all international flights. The atmosphere made even Ben forget her anger, and, for the first time, she began to feel some happiness, mixed with nervousness about the departure procedures they would soon undergo.

'Did you sleep well last night?' Ben asked her sister.

'Not really,' Ali answered.

'I didn't sleep well either,' Ben admitted.

Together with their agent, Hammond, they stopped at Etihad Airways check-in desk 4 after briefly waiting in a queue, 'Your passports and tickets please,' asked the female attendant at her desk.

After a careful check, she issued their boarding passes, and they proceeded to the security check. They placed their bags on the carousel. *Ali* and *Ben* were amazed at the swift services being provided, and they quickly responded to the caution, 'You are not supposed to take razors, scissors, nail cutters, or water bottles in your hand luggage.'

Ali got rid of her nail cutter and a bottle of Coca-Cola she had in her handbag. 'Remember, boarding starts in one hour and twenty minutes,' the gentleman who checked their boarding passes told them.

The girls spent an hour of their waiting time watching the countless passengers going about their departure formalities.

Some were carried away by emotions as they bid final goodbyes to their loved ones, amid tears.

Meanwhile, Mr Hammond engaged in a dialogue with a stocky middle-aged man wearing an all-grey suit. The two men spoke at length in Arabic, their tone low. Though the Almonds could hear them, they couldn't make out what the men were saying.

What are they talking about? Ben wondered. Finally, she enquired of her sister what the conversation might be about.

'Oh, er—I think he is pulling some strings,' Ali said.

'You know, he might be working on what we need to do to get through successfully.' She paused and added, 'So far, so good, huh? I think I'm impressed.

He seems good at what he does best, Ben thought.

Her thoughts were suddenly washed away, as a group of students on a transit to Beirut started singing and dancing while they waited for boarding to proceed. Neither sister could hide her joy as they took in the excitement.

The microphone suddenly buzzed, announcing, 'The 14.05 p.m. Etihad Flight 0119 is boarding at gate six.' The announcement was repeated in Arabic and French.

The sisters stood up, looked around, but could not find the architect of their trip. Suddenly, they heard a call behind them. 'Hey! Let's get on board.' They turned and, to their relief, saw Mr Hammond.

Ali, excited to seeing their agent, cried out, 'Hammond!'

'Come on. Let's go,' he ordered the girls, who could not hide their excitement as they climbed on board. They carefully stacked their hand baggage in the overhead cabin and got comfortably seated in the middle exit lane closest to the lavatory.

Soon, the in-flight screen switched on, and the flight safety demonstrations filled the screen. As the plane was an airbus, two flight attendants stood on either side of the aisles gesturing as the images played on the video screen and the instructions, in both English and Arabic, played over the public address system.

The crew completed instructions on the use of the seatbelts.

Then *Ali* and *Ben* quietly looked on as the brace position was displayed, followed by the image of the oxygen mask. At this stage, the plane had begun to taxi down the runway. 'Life vest are under your seats,' the public address system echoed. The explanation of emergency exits and the evacuation drills ended with a final reminder. 'Please, no smoking on board, including in the toilets. Please turn off all electric devices for take-off.' The video screen then went off.

The pilot's voice came over the public address system, 'Cabin crews, get ready for take-off.'

Etihad Flight 0119 to Singapore finally jumped into the air, to the delight of the sisters. Mr Hammond soon started snoring. The entire journey of six hours passed without the least turbulence. The plane also landed without any troubles. The girls and their agent booked reservations to stay in the transit lounge of Changi International Airport for six hours before connecting to JAL Flight 781 to Narita, Japan.

The Changi Airport was a major aviation hub in Asia, about twelve miles away from the city centre. 'I wish we could go out and take a look at the city,' Ben said.

'Yeah, I wish we could too, but we can't because we only have a transit visa allowing us to stay in the airport,' Mr Hammond reminded them.

'It seems like it would be a nice city, by the look of the airport design,' *Ali* said curiously.

Mr Hammond, clearing his throat, nodded and said, 'Yeah, it is. I have been once on business. It's a tiny island that has been transformed to a tropical paradise with nice casinos like in Las Vegas.'

Peeping through the transparent windows, *Ben* noticed that every passing car outside the airport drove with its windows shut. After a moment, she said out loud, 'I guess it might be very hot out there.'

'Yes it is—very hot, about 38° Celsius,' Hammond answered sharply.

I did not ask you any question, Ben thought, refusing to respond or even turn to look him in the face.

Eighteen

Barely two hours after arriving at the Kanfee transit lounge, despite all the excitement and the conversation, the girls gave way to the exertions of the journey. Ali started to snore, and soon afterwards, Ben also settled into a calm sleep.

'Hi, girls, can we go now?' asked Hammond, who had taken leave of them but had come back to see the girls still soundly asleep. He shook both of them, calling their names.

'We should be boarding now.'

The girls hurriedly picked up their hand baggage and made their way, following close behind him. Ali yawned and rubbed her hand over her eyes. 'Finally we are getting close to the dream of England,' she said softly.

Her sister, also in a bit of a haze for lack of enough sleep, smiled and nodded. They joined the queue for the final security checks before boarding.

Mr Hammond, leading the girls, was the first to be searched.

Suddenly he cried, 'Ah, my handbag. I will catch up with you guys on board soon.' Quickly, he retreated, heading back towards the Kanfee lounge to retrieve his handbag.

Ali was the next in line to be searched. 'Please put your bag on the carousel and take any metal objects, belts, or liquids out of your bag,' the friendly-looking male security guard instructed.

She did accordingly and stepped through the scanners successfully. Beaming a smile, she went to the end of the conveyor belt and stuffed her items into her handbag, as *Ben* followed the same instructions.

A guard came running towards *Ben* after her bag went though the scanner. He uttered a word that the girl could not understand. She ignored him and stepped over to take her bag. Then two uniformed policemen approached her.

'Miss, is this bag yours?' one asked her politely.

They asked her to wait as the bag was searched further.

Every item was once again taken out of the bag. Carefully, they used a razor to cut out the bottom lining of her bag.

She wondered in annoyance what was going on. She looked over at her sister, who was also watching the scene, clearly perplexed.

The inspection was taking longer than Ben thought it should, so she started to wander towards the waiting elder sister. But she was ordered, 'Please don't move!' The order was rather harsh, to the discomfort of the Almonds.

Then of all of a sudden, the passengers in queue behind Ben, as well as those who had already gone through the security check, including Ali, were confronted with shock—as a 5 mm shotgun was retrieved from Ben's handbag.

The number of police increased as reports of a suspected terrorist arrest swept through the airport. This place had been the scene of another female terrorist suspect arrest a week earlier, when a young female close to the same age as Ben confessed to an attempt to smuggle a gun on board to aid the blowing up of flight CX018.

No, this cannot be happening, Ben thought as police officers began to swarm the scene.

'Where did you get this from?' asked one of the officers.

'The gun looks real, and it seems to be loaded,' reported another.

'Oh wait,' she said and turned to look for Mr Hammond.

She glanced through the queue behind her but found no sign of him. She started to weep, calling to her sister, who was standing in shock, unable to say anything.

Ben turned around again agitatedly and yelled at her sister to come and tell them of her innocence.

Two police officers promptly moved towards *Ali* and asked, 'Are you two together?'

Ali grasped her hand baggage from the floor and said, 'Please, no.' She started to move away towards the boarding gate. When the restrained sister yelled again for the second time, "please do not leave me here" *Ali* felt cold blood flush through her heart, and she slowed. She thought "the police might probably arrest me for being her sister"

This worsen her fears. Silently, miserably, fearing the worst she doubled her pace hoping to find Mr Hammond to go back and help her poor sister.

Ben yelled through her tears, 'Ali! Ali!'

'Do you know her?' the police officer standing nearest Ben asked her.

'Yes, *he's* my *brother*' she wailed amidst tears.

Ben persistently refused to betray her sister by referring to Ali as 'Yes, *he's* my *brother*'. Ben has exonerated Ali and hence concealed her true feminine identity Once again, an officer stopped Ali and questioned *him* about *his* relationship to Ben.

'No,' *he* insisted, shaking *his* head. 'I only met *her* on the flight. I—don't know *her*,' *he* concluded.

As Ben intended and concealed the disguise of her sister, Ali unable to think straight, thus addressed her little sister as *her*, revealed the true identity of Benatu

As the officer allowed *Ali* to go, another ordered *Ben,* 'Put your hands behind you now!'

As soon as *Ben* complied, she felt handcuffs slapped around her wrists.

As she walked towards her boarding gate, *Ali* listened to her sister's frightened cries. *Ben* called her name over and over, yelling, 'Please don't leave me.' Ignoring the dreadful feelings that washed over her, she stoutly refused to look back and walked straight on the plane and took her seat on JAL flight 0781.

Ali's thoughts ran through what had just happened over and over. She waited impatiently for Hammond to turn up, knowing he was the only one who could possibly help her poor sister. Without her noticing, the plane had begun to taxi down the runway.

'Can you fasten your seatbelt for take-off, please,' a flight attendant told her.

The flight took off without any sign of Hammond on board.

It became apparent to *Ali* that Hammond had been around for all the wrong reasons and he had carefully covered his tracks, thus landing her only remaining sister into a horror she could not imagine.

*   *   *

Ben's true identity as a female was unraveled.

She was led out of the airport and put in a prisoners' van. Her thoughts returned to how the gun had gotten into her bag. She hadn't noticed anything unusual about her bag; she couldn't figure out how that gun had gotten there.

She still could not believe what had just happened, and then she was led through the entrance of the Gantabu medium-security prison. Inside was dark and damp, and the air was filled with unpleasant human smells. She reached for her nose but quickly pulled her hand back, for fear of repercussions.

Unlike the better populated immigration detentions she had been held at on many occasions, the prisoners here were nothing more than a conglomerate of crazy people, she soon realized. They clanged the iron bars and shouted their joy and anger at her.

As a female prisoner, she was subjected to screams of unknown dialect and obscene gestures. She could not look up for a second. Her ears clogged with the hisses and other noises.

No one looked friendly to her. She felt sick to her stomach when she was pushed into her cell and the iron bars hissed loudly and then slammed shut.

The first night was long, and her misery was worsened when the lights went out. The murmuring and occasional shouts continued late into the night. She woke up the next morning and further faced the reality of her dilemma in an eight-foot Gantabu cell. There was nothing to look at to reduce her stress or boredom; she could only stare at the same four concrete walls, and the tedium was overwhelming.

Barely twenty-four hours later, Benatu could think of nothing other than relishing the chance to take revenge on her sister, Mr Hammond, the desert thugs, and the Maltese man, Antonio, who she strongly believed knew the whereabouts of her lost sister, Taba.

Every day, Ben would wake at dawn, keeping faith that someone would come and get her out. She would wake before anyone else and would be the last to briefly nod into sleep.

She could not recall how many days she had spent in that solitary confinement, when she suddenly woke to the sound of the opening door. She was led away into a much bigger cell and left in the company of two other female inmates.

Both women were covered in blankets and lying on their beds. They looked at her intently. Benatu made no comment but marched in and sat quietly in the opposite corner. After a few minutes had passed, she managed to gaze up briefly; her heart leapt as she beheld both women still staring at her in silence.

She quickly thought, *What can I do to appease these restless cellmates?*

She lowered her gaze, but she could tell by the brief look at their faces that the one lying below might be a native, and the other—which she guessed by the paleness of her white skin—might be a European.

Surprisingly, the women never taunted her, and she, in turn, never spoke a word to her cellmates. Benatu knew for certain that she was in real trouble. Her memory went blank when both women got out of their beds and stood in front of her. The sheer size of the women made her cringe; her body shivered in alarm as her cellmate told her the rules governing the jail. She remembered almost nothing of what she heard, but the woman's final phrase kept ringing in her mind. 'There is something about this place, and those who simply do not speak will end up abused.'

A few hours later, she was taken out and led through a small corridor into another small cell, where she was met with a stiff smile. A young lady in an all-black suit with a pen in her hand started writing as soon as Benatu was led in. She wrote unceasingly as she asked Ben countless questions.

'Hello, have a seat,' the woman said to her as the guard walked out of the room. 'I am Kaolin Phua Chu, your lawyer; I am here to defend you, so whatever you tell me is confidential. Don't hesitate to tell me the truth.'

Tell you what truth? Benatu thought wearily.

The unassuming lawyer was quick to tell her client, 'I am from the chamber called the Gurus. I am appointed by the state to defend you.'

Benatu, who had grown up in a country where such rights could only be dreamt of, was at least glad to have legal representation, despite her loss of hope.

'I have no idea how the gun got into my bag,' Benatu said briefly.

'How did you acquire the bag?' her lawyer asked.

'Mr Hammond—I mean we gave him the money, and he bought it for us,' she said.

'Did you say for us?' asked the lawyer.

'Yes, I was travelling together with my sister and Mr Hammond, our agent.'

The lawyer urged her on, and she gave a full account of what had happened.

'How old are you now?'

'I turned seventeen the day I was arrested,' she said.

'But your passport shows that you are twenty?'

She lowered her gaze for a while and looked back into her lawyer's eyes. 'My agent told me my age needed to be increased to enable me to work full-time when we get to Japan,' she said. 'He said that people under eighteen could only work part-time.'

The lawyer paused briefly and nodded her head. She had been trained not to let her emotion rule her. She quickly summed up her notes and asked for the guards. 'Take care, Miss Benatu,' she said. 'I will see you very soon.'

Benatu was given a blanket and taken back to cell number 89.

Nineteen

Benatu had already spent a few hours with her two cellmates, and nothing harrowing had happened to her. However, their sudden movements and the appearance of the two women, who she did not yet know, frightened her to the spine.

One of the woman stood still, and her counterpart, who kept her eyes open but lay on her bed, made no sound. Five minutes passed, but none of them said anything.

Benatu could sense that something was not right. The women only gazed at her without blinking their eyes. Her cellmates increasingly mesmerising contemplation of her body made her look behind her for any possible retreat, but the perfectly shut, ugly painted iron doors made her cringe quietly.

Her breath increased as she restlessly waited for the onslaught. Interestingly, the woman on her feet finally slumped into her bed in tears.

In every jail the world over, there is an inmate or two who have influence over the rest, and here this happened to be Benatu's two cellmates, Adiza and Andrana.

Something about Benatu's charm made Adiza, who was six feet tall and heavily built, like the little girl at first sight.

Both women stood at six feet, but Andrana was a bit smaller in body size and was the younger of the two.

Andrana introduced herself to Benatu. She started in a language that Benatu didn't recognize. The little girl shook her head and gestured to her ears.

Andrana paused and took another look at Benatu. 'English?' she asked.

'Yes, please,' Benatu replied.

Andrana nodded her head and smiled wearily. 'I am thirty-six years old,' she said, 'and I have been here for eleven years.'

She paused and smiled at Benatu and asked, 'Can you guess why I was brought to jail?'

Benatu tried to make her voice sound normal. She shook her head and said, 'I have no idea.'

Adiza, who could be best described as thick, was forty; having spent twenty years of her life in that cell, everything about her looked a bully. 'What brings you here, little girl?' she asked.

Benatu yawned and said, 'I was arrested when a gun was found in my bag on our way to Japan.'

'What was your thought when you were arrested? Why did you have a gun?'

The sheer size of Adiza was enough to intimidate Benatu.

She calmly replied. 'No. I did not do it.'

'Did you meet your lawyer?' Adiza asked.

'Yes,' she answered. 'She said she works with a firm called the Gurus, and the law school she attended was—er—'

Benatu stopped, unable to recall the name the lawyer had given her.

'Which law school did she say?' her cellmate pressed.

'Er—something like—' She paused for a while, trying to remember. 'Samusun,' she finally said.

'Oh, right, Samusun Law School?' Her pale but bulky-looking cellmate seemed to be excited.

Benatu looked on confused. 'Why?' she asked.

The woman smiled again and shook her head and, in a disillusioned voice, said, 'Look, Samusun is the alma mater of many prominent lawyers in this country. My dad and mum were there, my elder sister was there, and I was there as well.'

*　　*　　*

After a week in the company and protection of her two strong cellmates, Benatu, the seventeen-year-old migrant, was bundled into the court building in shackles and in full view of the media.

She was brought before the Central Court in Singapore charged with plotting to hijack a plane and crash it into Singapore's Changi Airport and conspiracy to commit terrorist acts in the country.

The display was intended to convey the impression that Benatu was a highly dangerous young woman, like several men charged with terrorist offences around the world over the past years.

I *am innocent. I have nothing to fear*, she thought. However, her experience in the courthouse was rather an odder one than she had expected.

As soon as she was bundled into the courtroom, heads swivelled and necks craned. She courageously looked up and scanned the public gallery, hoping she might see her sister or someone else there for her to rely on. She instead noticed that the people in the public gallery started nudging each other and pointing and whispering.

She knew what they were talking about. *I am a terrorist*, she thought. Her heartbeat raced as she soon took note of someone commenting lewdly, 'Terrorist.'

The physical appearance of the High Court in Central Singapore, although tidy, was cramped and the furnishings were old. The wooden benches in the public gallery creaked nosily with every movement of the body.

The bench of three all-male High Court judges, presumably in their late sixties, were already seated on their chairs on a high platform in front of the courtroom.

Also present in the courtroom were two female clerks, one in black gown and a white wig and the other in an all-black suit seated on the right-hand side next to the judges. The others, who sat below in the judge's bench, were the only people moving around in the courtroom. On the far right three rolls of empty wooden benches were occupied by the press, instead of jurors.

Benatu was led in her shackles straight into the defendant's dock, located right in the middle of the courtroom. With four police guards around her, the 'mitten handcuffs', which were intended to prevent criminals from being able to grab an object, such as an officer's gun, were unlocked. She felt relieved to be released from the rigid grip. She looked at her wrists briefly, and then gently she rubbed her palms around her wrists.

While her hands were left free, her legs were still fettered, and the restriction on her movement made her feel sick.

Her ankles remained in the rigidly designed ratchet cuffs.

Although their rigid design and the inclusion of a grip make it effective for gaining control over a struggling prisoner, its usage had been widely condemned, even in medieval times.

The male barrister representing the prosecution, who looked to be in his forties, sat beside the public attorney who had visited and was representing Benatu.

At just about 11.00 a.m., the proceedings started. The court usher pronounced Benatu's full name—'Benatu Almond'—to the court and listed the charges against her. She was then asked, 'Miss Benatu Almond, are you guilty of the charges against you?'

Without hesitation, she spoke into the microphone arranged before her. 'Innocent.'

The legal proceedings started with the defence counsel standing and making her opening speech, while the judges remained quiet and seated. The opening speech was quite short.

The real evidence of the case—Benatu's bag and the gun retrieved from her bag—were exhibited to the court. These were passed on and vigorously examined by the bench of judges.

Benatu was questioned. She told the court that she had not put the gun in her bag and alleged that her agent might have possibly placed it in her bag.

The prosecution barrister objected to that and circulated a picture of the defendant clutching onto her bag at the airport prior to their pre-departure security check.

Benatu's defense lawyer, Kaolin Phua Chu, took some time to ask her client, the defendant, some questions. She asked, 'Miss Benatu, how old are you?'

'Seventeen, please,' Ben answered.

The prosecution lawyer rose up sharply from his seat and roared, 'Objection, my lord; she is twenty years old, and I have the facts to prove that.'

There was evidence of a smoothly functioning courtroom, as the judges closely monitored the proceedings without unnecessary interruptions.

'Objection sustained,' one of the judges proclaimed. He added that not until Miss Kaolin Phua Chu could show any evidence to dispute the age of her client according to the client's passport would the court accept any verbal pleadings otherwise.

Benatu's attorney then asked her to narrate her account of the story to the court, which she did without hesitation, maintaining that she was innocent.

She was surprised when her defence lawyer asked her to tell the court of her previous convictions. She responded without hesitation that she had never been arrested for a crime. The relevance of this question suddenly became clear, as the defence lawyer gave credibility to the defendant's testimony and backed it by presenting all the relevant information to verify that, throughout her life, her client had never been arrested or charged, neither in her home country of Somalia or abroad. As such, the attorney concluded, she had been a victim of human traffickers.

The defence attorney further argued that the defendant's age should be considered, as she was still less than eighteen years old. She asserted that, in addition, there had been no apparent social class of the defendant that would link her to any evil groups. Miss Kaolin Phua Chu concluded that her client had been very cooperative with the police investigation, indicating that she was innocent.

Benatu felt some liberation as some of the judges nodded their heads in appreciation of Phua Chu's concluding argument.

In the end, the prosecuting barrister brought forth further evidence against the defendant and asked Benatu, 'Do you know one Chichipa Hammidu?'

'No, I've never heard that name,' Ben replied.

'Are you not associated with the terrorist group known as Al bi Jibar?'

Again Benatu answered, 'I have never heard of it.'

The prosecuting lawyer paused and said to the defendant, 'I have facts to prove that you have and that you and your alleged alibi known as Mr Hammond were affiliated with this group in both Arabia and Northern Libya.

'You have been to Libya and Arabia right?'

'Yes,' she answered.

He then reached out for his file and exhibited five pictures to the court, which showed images of Benatu and her sister, together with Hammond and some other men in Arabia.

He went on to tell the court that the other two men found in the picture with Benatu were both top members of the

Al bi Jibar movement. Both had since been arrested, found guilty, and were awaiting the gas chamber in California.'

Benatu's heart sunk over this new evidence against her, as she was handed the pictures. *Oh my God*, she said to herself. She told the court that yes, the pictures were of her, her sister, and Mr Hammond. But she denied knowing the two other men. She further explained that she had only met the two men at a dinner dance organized by the high commissioner of Somalia, who was a friend of Mr Hammond.

The prosecution counsel then took the stage to make his closing speech. He referenced Singapore Justice and Terrorism Act of 1998. He urged the judges not to disregard the pictures he'd circulated and to decide the case solely on the evidence provided by the prosecution counsel. He concluded that it was the duty of the prosecution to bring evidence against the defendant, and this had been done. He had proved the accused guilty beyond reasonable doubt. As such, the maximum sentence should be carried out.

Then the defence counsel made her closing statement.

'My lord,' she began, 'I would plead a case of an innocent girl who was naive and too young to realize the dangerous people around her. The only problem is that the gun was found in her bag. She does not deny that. It is clear that she had no idea how the gun ended up in her bag. And almost all the evidence put before the court has confirmed her story. Therefore, my client will still plead innocent.'

The summing up was done by each of the judges, since Benatu's was a trial without jury. Each pointed out that the Arms Offences Act, which regulated firearms offences, provided that any person convicted of arms use or of being an accomplice to a person convicted of arms use during a scheduled offence could be executed.

At this juncture, a verdict was read. 'Guilty and to be executed by rope; no room for appeal.'

Benatu's guilty verdict made the headlines; a picture of her in tears appeared in the national newspaper and was posted on a Yahoo page.

Twenty

For the entire journey, Alima could think only of the arrest of her younger sister. Jet-lagged and having been unable to sleep on board, she finally arrived in Tokyo on the morning of 11 September 1995.

Despite being jet-lagged, exhausted, and disoriented, she surprisingly warmed towards the immigration and customs procedures, after which a photograph of her and her fingerprints were taken. 'Okay, goodbye. Have a nice stay in Japan,' she was told.

She walked toward the carousel to collect her luggage. 'I can't believe I am in Japan,' she whispered to herself.

She felt certain as her purple backpack bounced down the carousel and she stepped forward to pick it up. But a middle-aged Asian man in a purple suit with a red necktie caught her eye. *Did I see this man on the flight?* she tried to recall. *No, I don't think so.*

She pulled her bag from the carousel in haste. With no idea of a possible destination, she paused for a moment. In fear of being found loitering, she made up her mind and headed towards the toilet. A few metres before the entrance to the female toilet, she paused and glanced back. She stiffened with fear as the man in the purple suit turned the corner, in pursuit of her as she had feared.

She increased her pace and headed towards the toilet. She slowed and glanced back again. The man had moved closer, and to her horror she caught the man's gaze and he smiled at her, showing two golden front teeth. It would be very unusual for her to take to her heels, so she doubled her steps, walked into the restroom and into one of the stalls, and pushed the door shut.

'Oh my god, who is this man?' she whispered to herself.

She could feel her heartbeat race. She waited for about five minutes before stepping out carefully and scanning her surroundings for any hint of the colour purple. She sighed with relief as the man seemed to have disappeared.

She walked towards the international arrival exit with other arriving passengers.

The exit hall was packed with anticipated arrivals, some hugging and kissing their loved ones in delight, others shedding tears of joy. With no destination in mind, she slowed her steps and remembered a story Mr Hammond had told them about a Japanese woman called Kauri from a town called Isesaki in Guma, who would be meeting them at the airport as their host.

She could only draw an imaginary picture of the woman in the crowded arrival hall. In anticipation that this might be her host, she smiled willingly at almost any middle-aged female who took a second glance at her. She made her way to the end of the hall with no sign of any Kauri. *What should I do now?* she wondered.

She hurriedly searched her wallet and pulled out some U.S. dollar bills. In the process, a coin dropped and rolled behind her. Gazing down, her focus on the rolling coin, she turned only to find a purple-suited figure right behind her. Never raising her head to look him in the face, she avoided the coin and moved away.

Clutching her backpack tightly and pulling her small suitcase, she made her way towards the exit that showed the JR train logo.

'Alima,' she heard. She saw two men displaying a placard with the words, 'Welcome Alima', written on it.

The men approached her, beaming with smiles. Both were nearly of the same height—about five foot seven. The one carrying the placard around his neck was wearing an all-grey suit tailored in pure Italian perfection and a pink shirt underneath without a necktie. A matching hat of one of the finest Panama Bosalino was flawlessly perched atop his head.

The other, who spoke not a word but only offered brief smiles, was in a black suit with a black shirt and a black tie to match. The sides of his head were shaved, and he wore a ponytail tied in the back.

Who are these guys? she thought, not forgetting her fear of being stalked by the man in purple. She slowed and smiled back at the men. 'Who are you?' she asked in English.

They paused and, rather awkwardly, the one in the grey suit replied in Japanese. She didn't have a clue what he'd said.

Uncomfortable, Alima decided to walk on.

Then, the man with the ponytail whispered in her ear, 'Yes, my friend is Mr Hammond. We can help you.'

She felt her body fill with intense hatred at the mention of Mr Hammond.

But I need help anyway, she thought wearily. She looked away briefly as her younger sister's nightmare rushed back to fill her mind. She rigidly raised her head and shook it, tilting it backwards to keep the drops of tears in her eyes from falling.

The men persisted in smiling at her. Then all of a sudden,

Alima felt a tap on her left shoulder. As she turned towards the sound of a low voice, she froze in fear; she was face-to-face with the man in the purple suit. He had been stalking her all along.

He spoke in rather clear English. 'Come with us. We are good men. We can help you. Hammond is our good friend.'

He smiled widely, showing three golden teeth. Offering his hand for a handshake, he said, 'My name is Mr Miyazaki, and'—he pointed to the other two guys, indicating first the man with the ponytail—'this is Mr Kobayashi, and this is Mr Salto.'

All three men smiled and offered to carry her bag.

Okay, she thought, at last regaining some sort of composure, *I think I should ask them about our missing agent.* 'Where is Mr Hammond then?' she enquired.

'Er—he called us,' Mr Miyazaki replied. 'He said that he missed the flight when he rushed to look for one of his lost bags, so we should take care of you.'

'Right,' she replied. 'When is he coming then?'

'Next Monday at 6.00 a.m., on the same flight,' Mr Miyazaki answered sharply, without looking at her.

'Where are we going now?' she enquired.

'Now? Er—we are going to Kobe,' he replied.

Mr Salto led the way, grabbing her little suitcase and moving towards the exit gate, while Mr Kobayashi pleaded with her to let go of the backpack she clutched firmly to her chest.

Suddenly, a woman shouted at the top of her voice, 'No,

Alima, I am here. I am Kauri. Mr Hammond told you about me, right?'

As the two women tried to greet each other, Mr Miyazaki instructed Salto to assist Kobayashi in pulling the backpack from Alima's grip. A tussle ensued, as the three men ignored the suitcase on the floor and became determined to snatch away the backpack Alima was carrying.

Two uniformed policemen on patrol stepped towards them swiftly. '*Douh shta?*'—*meaning what is amiss?* one of them asked.

Kobayashi, without hesitation, introduced himself to the policemen. 'Hi, no problem,' he said. 'I'm Kobayashi, and these two young men are my boys.' He cleared his throat and went on. 'My client rang me up from Singapore and asked me to meet this lady, who would be delivering his backpack to us at the airport.' He paused and smiled suspiciously and concluded by saying, 'So we are only here to collect our client's bag from this lady called Alima.'

'I guess you are Alima-san, right?' one of the policemen asked in English.

She nodded. 'Yes I am, but this bag is not Mr Hammond's, and he did not ask me to deliver it to anyone.'

'All right. I think there is some confusion here. Let's move to the police post to solve this issue,' the policemen pleaded gently.

'No,' Mr Kobayashi answered sharply. 'We are not moving anywhere. We just need our client's bag.'

In fear of violence, the officer radioed for backup, and more policemen soon arrived.

One of them asked, 'What is in the bag?'

'My clothes,' Alima answered.

'Well let's check what exactly is in the bag.' the policeman insisted.

She promptly dropped the bag on the floor, unzipped it, and started to empty its contents.

My Kobayashi walked over to Sato and whispered something into his ear.

Mr Salto responded and walked towards the policemen.

'*Summimasen, machigaita desu*—mistake.' He paused then spoke again, 'Mistake, sorry.' He explained that they were waiting for Amina not Alima.

One of the police officers stopped Alima when she was halfway through emptying the bag. 'Okay, you can go.'

She gladly stood up and warmed towards her new friend, Kauri-san.

Within minutes, the three men had bowed apologetically and hurriedly disappeared towards the exit B car park.

What was all that about? Alima wondered. The three men had seemed to genuinely know Mr Hammond and all the details of his trip.

Twenty One

'You must be tired. Come with me,' Kauri said.

Alima followed her back into the arrival hall. 'Where are we going again?' Alima asked.

They came to a counter behind which a woman stood. She smiled at them and uttered something in Japanese. Kauri spoke to the woman briefly then paid her some Japanese yen and was issued with a receipt. Then a man stepped over from the counter to pick up Alima's bag.

Alima, unable to understand what was going on, blocked the man from taking her luggage.

'Ah it is fine. This is Takiyoubi,' Kauri alleged, turning towards Alima to explain. 'No worries. Give them all the bags. They will be delivered to us at home tonight.'

With some hesitation, Alima let go of her bags.

They headed to the JR train station, where Alima was amazed by the efficiency of the countless little ticket vending machines at the station. She watched on curiously as Kauri inserted a note and two tiny paper tickets popped out. A second later, she smiled in surprise when she saw that the exact change dropped out in coins.

The first thing Alima noticed when the Keisei line limited express train approached the platform was how clean and new it looked. She stepped into the train behind Kauri and sat right beside her on the third carriage.

'How was your trip?' Kauri requested.

'It was—er, fine.' she responded and kept her silence again, to the discomfort of her host. Wondering about her sister's ordeal, she has become apprehensive of any associates of Hammond. The train ride was smooth, to Alima's delight, and she fell asleep shortly after boarding.

Midway into the journey, she awoke and rubbed her hands hurriedly over her eyes to get rid of the sleep.

'It has become so crowded now,' she said.

Kauri, relieved to see Alima awake, answered with a smile.

'Oh yes, that's normal from this station onwards.' She offered Alima a soft drink called Pocari Sweat.

'Thank you,' Alima said, taking the bottle and greedily drinking from it. She stretched her body and turned towards Kauri. 'I feel better now,' she said. 'How long will it take to get to your place?'

'In the next ten minutes, we'll have to change trains and, from there, it will be another thirty minutes until we get to my place,' Kauri answered. 'I think you might be hungry.

We will get something to eat soon,' she added.

On arrival at Ueno, they headed for dinner in a local Japanese pub called Izakaya. Alima wondered what type of food would be there. *Thankfully*, she thought as she saw that the entire menu was covered with large pictures of the dishes the pub served.

She ordered a steaming bowl of *lamen*, which she devoured without hesitation. Not satisfied, her host invited her to walk through the market to look for a sushi bar.

They headed through the popular fish market. Alima stopped and yelled in odd-sounding voice, 'Look at those, er—all those countless snake-shaped creatures.' She turned towards her host and smiled, pointing at the eels making fruitless leaping attempts to rise over each other and the walls of their containers, each bids for escape a foregone failure.

The giant octopuses did not escape her attention either.

'Wow!' she yelled. 'Look at that huge lobster.' There were varieties of fish she could never have imagined. In nearly every stall, she saw different kinds of fresh fish. Some were still flapping their gills. She felt greatly satisfied, as she gazed at all around her in wonderment.

The chain of restaurants lining the streets near the fish market seemed the perfect place to stop for some sushi.

Having been told that sushi was made from raw fish, Alima was curious to find out what it tasted like.

Again she gazed at the pictures on the menu. Everything looked rather strange to her, so she told Kauri, 'I will just have the same thing that you eat.'

'Why? Are you sure?' Kauri inquired.

'Yeah, just order anything. I'll be fine,' Alima assured her.

The order came with an array of varieties on a big white plate—two portions each of tuna, salmon, and crab nigiri. She frowned at the sea urchin nigiri, which looked suspiciously shady; it was yellow, like mustard.

'This is about doing new things in a new country, and sushi is the symbol of Japanese food,' Kauri told her.

They soon ate everything on the plate. 'It's pretty good!'

Alima exclaimed. Even the sea urchin, which she tasted at the end of the meal, was surprisingly tolerable.

Finally, they took a local bus home. Kauri ushered her into her room in the basement; it was quite small but very tidy.

She headed into the bathroom with her towel and sponge.

The toilet sink adjacent to the bathroom was very clean but very small. *My late mum would surely not fit in this toilet,* she thought.

Where should I stand? She marvelled at the size of the bathroom, and what was strangest of all was the small bath referred to in Japanese as *ohuro*. She guided herself through the shower and was soon sleeping deeply in the bed she'd been offered in the basement room.

She slept from 4.00 p.m. until 2.00 a.m. She awoke and found her luggage on a table in her room. She staggered upstairs to the living room, where she found Kauri and her elder sister, Kimie, happily competing against each other in a Pokemon video game.

'Ah, *okita*!'—Kimie exclaimed on seeing Alima.

'You're up now. Did you sleep well?' Kauri asked her.

She nodded, but still jet-lagged and feeling drowsy, she made her way through the doors to the tiny balcony. The view from the balcony made her feel suddenly awake; little red lights glowed from the tops of the other buildings all around her.

Everything around her seemed cute and stylish. She touched the cute stylish clothing hanging on the balcony.

As she walked back into the living room, she smiled at the globe-shaped fluorescent light bulb in the room. *Everything looks so different*, she deliberated.

'We want to go and get some food. Would you come with us?' Kauri inquired.

'Yes, I will,' Alima replied, but she was surprised by the request when she glanced at the time. It was ten passed two.

She dressed up quickly, and off they went in Kimie's car.

The drive was rather short but, Alima could not take her eyes off the night's sea of lights that stretched out in the horizon in all direction. After a five-minute drive, they got out of the car in front of a convenience shop.

'This place is called Tenjin,' Kauri told her.

Alima saw a lot of people around. On the other side of the road were shops, including a 7-eleven. On the other end were giant gleaming lights displaying a pachinko advertisement and a huge car park fully filled with cars. Adjacent to the pachinko billboard was another convenience shop with a bold sign, 'Family Mart.' Some of the people hurried with their purchases and sped off, while some younger customers leaned on their cars and chatted.

Alima looked at her watch again, thinking she might be confused about the time. She asked, 'Is it almost to 3.00 a.m.? Why are the shops open?'

'They offer twenty-four-hour service,' Kauri explained.

Alima looked around the shop. Only two young women, busily serving customers with smiles, were present. 'No security men?' she asked. 'Is that not risky?'

Kimie smile and said, '*Hewa*, Japan is peaceful,—no troubles here. Let's go,' she added.

They had almost made it back home when Kimie slowed.

'We forgot to buy drinks,' she said.

'Let's get some from those vending machines,' Kauri said.

Without hesitation, Kimie pointed her car in the direction Kauri had indicated, and they soon arrived at the vender.

Alima was further surprised at how easy it was to get alcohol, soft drinks, hot coffee, tobacco, ice cream, or even hot noodles from countless vending machines, apparently found all over the country.

In less than twenty-four hours, a place she had assumed she would despise suddenly became a special place in her heart.

She made her first trip to the heart of Tokyo the following afternoon. She enjoyed travelling through the port city of Yokohama and gazing up at all the buildings that seemed to go on and on. She turned in either direction to take in the sights, making her first day in Japan a memorable one.

She and Kauri took the metro to some historical areas around the Tokyo borough. An entrance gate into a Buddhist temple on the outskirt of the city was lined with the enormous hanging lanterns, which Alima found excessively exciting.

The scary statutes of the gods around the shiny gates of the pagoda reminded her of her native country.

'So when are you going back?' Kauri asked her

'What do you mean? Oh, you mean leaving Japan?' Alima enquired

'Er—yes. Mr Hammond told me you would only be staying for two weeks.'

'Have you heard from him lately?' Alima asked.

'Yes, we spoke on the phone this morning, and he reminded me of your duration of stay.'

Alima smiled and nodded her head, 'Right,' she said. 'When is he coming to Japan then?'

'I'm not sure, but he said he lost his bag containing a very important document. The bag was found this morning, so he'll probably be coming to Japan next week.'

Alima said nothing further.

Twenty Two

Barely a week into Alima's stay in Japan, she began to ponder where she would go next; she decided to take a walk in the neighbourhood alone. She hadn't gone far when she remembered she had no identification documents on her; she had been told to always be in possession of her passport to avoid any possible detention.

She walked back into her room, wondering what the relationship between Kauri and Mr Hammond might be.

Her bags still remained on the floor, with almost all her clothes intact.

She heard a knock on her door. 'Come in,' she responded.

Kauri entered. 'There is going to be a fire flower tonight at 7.00 p.m.,' she told Alima. 'Do you want to come with me?'

Alima responded cheerfully, 'Of course, yes. Is there any dress code?'

'Not really,' Kauri told her. 'You can wear anything. I will dress casually, but most Japanese will be in traditional kimonos.'

Alima hurried towards her bags, excited to look for something presentable to wear. She emptied the contents of her little suitcase on the bed and then she unzipped her backpack.

'You can arrange your clothes in that hanging oak double ladies wardrobe from Quebec if you want,' Kauri told her.

Alima again responded cheerfully.

As she emptied the remaining contents of her backpack, an object tightly fastened in a black cloth dropped from the bottom of the bag.

She paused curiously, picked it up, and untied it.

Underneath the cloth was a clear airtight plastic bag.

She stiffened at the sight of a Jericho 941 double action semi-automatic pistol loaded with 9×19mm Parabellum cartridge Alima froze. She returned in her mind to the airport. She whispered to herself, 'Son of a bitch.' This was precisely the same kind of gun found in Benatu's bag at the airport.

'Oh my God. What is this?' Kauri whispered in a voice full of fear and shock.

'What is that?' She demanded again when Alima did not reply. This time her tone was very angry. 'It's a gun, right!?'

Alima was speechless and only shook her head dejectedly.

Kauri stepped up and grasped the gun from Alima. She examined it down to the engraved serial number around the grip. She carefully looked at the trigger cocks; her heartbeat raced as she realized that the gun exactly fit to the shape of her hand.

Not for the faint-hearted or weak wristed, she thought sadly.

This is a monster double-action revolver meant to take peoples' lives. The visible and shining engraved serial number on the gun suggested to her that it had come straight from the factory.

Without further hesitation, she turned to her guest. 'Alima, I want you to leave this house now!'

'Can I explain something to you, please?' Alima pleaded.

'No! Please go away now before I call the police,' Kauri roared at her, amid tears.

Alima looked into Kauri's face. She wished she could at least ask her for a little money, but she was unable to ask as she discerned that her host's face had turned purple and her cheeks were bright red. She realized Kauri's deep anger could turn ugly at any further provocation. *She looks so different*, she thought.

Without further comment, Alima hurriedly packed her belonging into her bags and dashed out into the darkness, watching her back with agitation at the sound of every movement of passing cars.

She walked briskly for about an hour. She felt very uncomfortable, as every passerby and every passenger in every car that crossed her path seemed to stare at her.

She came to a halt near the convenient shop where she'd gotten food with Kauri and her sister on her first night in the country in the Tenjin city centre. She had no destination in mind. *Oh how I wish I had never been born*, she reflected sadly.

A cheerfully young lady approached her and said to her, '*Konichiwa-hello* America, *jin deska?*'

Alima was taken aback, unsure exactly what the girl meant, but she forced a smile and nodded.

The girl smiled back and said, 'Ah, I love America. I love hip hop, Tupac, Usher, er—Miss Elliot.'

Alima quickly guessed what she meant. Although she associated the country called the USA with the artist Michael Jackson, she didn't know of any other artists from that place, let alone the numerous artists her aspiring friend had just mentioned.

How on earth does she know all these names? she wondered.

Alima, who had hailed from a village where only the king and two other prominent members of the village out of the 5,000 had access to a television or video set, was left speechless when the young girl tuned on a video of Usher's 'Confession' on her mobile phone.

Trying not to further embarrass herself, she gave a thumbs up in appreciation, smiled at the girl again, and started to walk on. She then stopped and asked herself, *But where am I going?*

With no particular destination in mind, she turned back towards her newfound friend, who had taken a turn and was waiting for a bus at a bus stop nearby.

'Hello, you speak English, right?' Alima asked.

The girl shook her head and said, 'Er, no, no; *ego Hanasemasen—cannot speak English* Using sign language and some English words, Alima made the girl understand that she wanted to get to the train station so she could catch a train to Tokyo. Without hesitation, the girl guided her to the train station, which was about 100 metres away.

After Alima's friend took leave of her, she checked her money against the ticket prices. She took a deep breath as disappointment filled her. The cost of ticket to the capital city was far higher than she'd expected and beyond her reach.

She remembered that she had a visa card, which she decided to use to withdraw some cash. She keyed in her pin number twice, but the cash machine rejected her card.

A few minutes passed, as she tried to think of what to do.

She adjusted her backpack properly on her back; clutched her little suitcase, which contained the gun, against her chest; and made her way to the ticket attendant.

'Hello, do you speak English?' she asked bodily.

To her relief, the attendant answered, 'Yes, a little.'

'Er, I have to get to Tokyo, but the ATM has rejected my card,' she told the man.

'Can I see the card please?' the attendant asked.

Alima handed over her blue visa card to the attendant, who looked at it for a while then said, 'Okay, I think it expired yesterday. That's why the machine won't take it.'

Alima sounded very genuine as she cried, 'Oh my God.

What is today's date?'

'Today is Friday, 19 September,' the attendant told her. 'But how will you pay if you get to Tokyo?'

'Without hesitation, she answered, 'My family is waiting at the station and will get me some money to pay.'

The ticket attendant became indecisive for a while and then dialled a phone number and spoke briefly to someone, listening for a moment and then responding with phrases such as '*Hai*! *Hai*!' Alima knew this meant *yes*, and she watched the attendant make occasional glances at her luggage.

This man might be reporting me to the police, she thought.

Unsure of who the man was talking to, she decided to walk away.

The attendant soon hanged up and called Alima back.

'Okay,' he said, 'my boss said okay, so we will give you a temporary pass. When you get to Shinjuku, please give it to the attendant and pay all right?'

She looked at the piece of paper in her hand scripted with a combination of hiragana, katakana, and the strangely weaved kanji. She warmly thanked him and made her way with the piece of paper onto the platform.

With no particular destination in mind, she boarded the Takasaki train line bound for Tokyo. She positioned herself near the windows and looked suspiciously at every passenger within her eyeshot, trying to guess at what would happen to her next.

An hour and a half later, she made her way out of the train at Shinjuku station. *What next?* she contemplated as she observed thousands of commuters rushing across platforms and train lines.

She stood still for a while, unable to figure out how to exit without paying. She decided to follow a sign that read, 'Toei Ōedo Line'. She headed onto platform two; soon, a train approached, and she quickly boarded it.

For the first time in the country, she observed some foreign faces on board the train. Some westerners were engaged in conversation.

'Jim, make sure you don't drink like you did last weekend,' one said.

The person Alima presumed to be Jim smiled at the rest and said nothing.

The train came to a stop at a station, and Alima noticed that all the westerners and the other ladies dressed up in miniskirts moved towards the exit. She also sprang up and joined them as they headed out of the train.

Clutching her backpack against her chest and the little suitcase in her hand, she walked towards the ticket inspector, waving her conditional ticket at the inspector. And to her surprise, the inspector opened up the automated barriers, allowing her to walk out.

She stepped out and stopped before the station coin locker, where she locked up her little case As she walked out, she looked back again and noted the station name—'Roppongi'.

This was an area that was well known for its variety of night life and foreign influence. Bars, nightclubs, and restaurants spiralled in all directions in regional rivalry.

It was thought the Japanese yakuza had, in recent times, shifted much of their presence to other districts in the Tokyo area, but the organized crime syndicates still exerted great influence in Roppongi.

Clubs ranged from large, multilevel establishments to smaller, one-room clubs located either in the upper levels of buildings or lower basements. Top of the top were the famous Yakuza-owned Kuabakuras and the popular Rock Cafe bar. The Lexington Queen was also one of the longest established Roppongi venues.

Twenty Three

As Alima took in the influx of younger crowds and the large non-Japanese community in the neighbourhood, she warmed to the place.

With her backpack now behind her, she made her way towards the Rock Cafe. She stopped and scanned the room, looking at the groups of coffee and Asahi drinkers enjoying each other's company and decided, 'No, this is not the place for me.'

She strolled in and out of about five free bars until she came to one with the Rastafarian colours of red, yellow, and green at the top and the inscription, 'Uprising Reggae Bar.'

She stepped into the lift in the company of two lovely Japanese girls and was met with the traditional cry of welcome, '*Irasshaimase*.'

Her first impression of the Uprising Bar was that it was a bit small, but the background music of Max Romeo soon made her nostalgic. She remembered that her dad had once told her, 'Hope is even greater than life. People go to bed with plans of what they will do the next day or days to come without any assurance that they will be alive the next day. All is based on hope.'

She gathered the necessary hope and beamed at the rather shy Japanese and some foreign nationals who were present.

She sat quietly, and when presented with the drink menu, she hesitated.

Before finally settling on orange juice, she felt as if someone was watching her. She looked up and found herself staring into the drunken eyes of six males, who jerked their necks to stare and admire her looks.

What are they looking at? she wondered.

A well-dressed Japanese woman took the last remaining seat next to Alima at the main counter. Alima didn't notice, as she remained preoccupied with the men who continued to stare at her and who she believed were sharing some gossip about her.

'Konichiwa,'—meaning hello, said a voice at her shoulder.

She looked up towards the person and smiled, shaking her head and signalling to her ears to indicate that she did not understand the language. The woman, who seemed rather interesting, spoke in English. 'Hello, my name is Shihor,' she said. 'Nice to meet you. Are you from America?'

Alima shook her head, indicating that she was not American.

There was a brief silence as she contemplated how to initiate the whole process of conversation or getting acquainted with this woman.

She wondered if it would be better to claim that she was an American or in order to gain the respect of the Japanese.

This was the sixth time she had been in conversation with natives and had seen that they seemed to take more delight in Americans than any other citizens. 'I am from Somalia,' she said.

'Somalia, where is that?' The woman paused then said, 'Brazil? America?' Her inquiry confirmed beyond a doubt that she had never heard of Somalia.

Alima, annoyed by the woman's lack of knowledge, forced a dry smiled and said, 'It in the Eastern part of Africa.'

'Oh right, Africa, *gin ka*,' the woman exclaimed. 'I would like to go, er—Safari in Africa,' she added.

Alima made no immediate comment. She smiled again in disappointment. A few seconds later, she reached out with her hand and said, 'Anyway, my name is Alima. Nice to meet you.'

The woman beamed back at Alima and said, 'My name Shihor means happy. I am very happy to meet you. Why are you in Japan? Are you a student? Or are you here on business?'

'No, just on holiday,' Alima answered sharply.

'Oh nice. Do you like it in Japan?'

'Yes, I like it,' Alima replied.

Alima sat sipping her orange juice with no any other plan in mind. She then decided to order a pint of beer. She felt tipsy as the minutes ticked into hours. She watched as night revellers poured in and out for drinks and fun. She glanced at her digital wristwatch. It was 1.00 a.m. She sighed. With an empty hope in the back of her mind, she decided it was time to go before she was asked to leave.

She dashed through the door onto the street, taking a few steps away from the reggae bar. She saw her new friend, Shihor, waving and strolling towards her, another nice-looking woman walking beside her. 'You don't have to go to your hotel,' Shihor invited. 'You can come with me to our house; my parents will be fine with that.'

Oh my God, Alima whispered inwardly. She wished she could just yell, *Yes, please, take me with you, for I need help.*' Alima could not pluck up the courage to do so. Instead, she smiled shyly at Shihor, pretending to shrug, and replied, 'I don't want to bother you guys. Are you sure your parents wouldn't have a problem with you bringing home a stranger?'

Both girls covered their mouths and laughed briefly, and then Shihor said to Alima, 'Please come with us. This is my little sister, Akemi.'

On their way to Shihor and Akemi's, Shihor, who was much more open than her little sister, told Alima that she just graduated from the Tsukuba Science University, where she had studied chemistry, and was looking forward to travelling around the world. She also wished to marry a foreigner.

'What is so special about a foreigner?' Alima asked politely.

'Er—' Shihor paused for a while and, again hiding her smile behind her palm, she said, 'Japanese men are cool, but foreign men are cool and more open-minded.

Then Akemi, who had not yet spoken a word, added that she was studying English and wanted to go to America or Australia to learn to speak better English.

Alima was filled with emotion as she listened to her age mates talk about their dreams and aspiration, whilst she was only trying to survive. Desperately needing a place to stay, Alima encouraged the two young women to talk about their dreams. They finally got to the sisters' home and, being careful not to disturb the sleeping household, they settled in quietly.

*   *   *

The house was surprisingly larger than Alima had thought it was when they'd first arrived in the night. She had been assigned a room, and for two weeks, neither of the girls nor their mother, who hadn't come out of her room since Alima had arrived, ever asked her when she would be leaving.

Their father was away on holiday.

However, on the third Monday, as Alima was cleaning her room, Shihor came in and said, 'My father came home last night, and he wants to speak to you.'

Alima blinked at the news. She felt her heartbeat amplified, and she anticipated the possibilities of eviction. She looked around nervously and curiously, as she followed her friend into the sitting room. She had never been into this part of the hall. It was very huge and bright. Despite her nervousness, Alima could not keep her eyes off the classic tapestries hanging all over the walls.

She was soon introduced to a woman who was reclined on a sofa, and Alima was surprised at how young Shihors's mum looked. The back door then opened. A short but heavily built man emerged. He had a ponytail with the side of his head shaved neatly to the skin. He had very strong and visible cheekbones. It was hard to tell his age, but the neatly trimmed silver moustache suggested that he was in his early fifties.

One look at the man brought a sharp hint of familiarity to her memory. Her heart sunk, but she could not remember where she had seen the man.

Shihor made the introduction quickly, in a rather nervous but soft voice, while Alima constantly looked down, her hands behind her.

There was a brief uneasy silence as the man eyed Alima up and down and then sighed audibly before stepping forward.

He addressed Alima in a reasonable tone. 'Your name is Alima, right?'

After a moment of hesitation, she answered, 'Yes please,' stumbling slightly.

The man stepped forward thoughtfully towards Alima without further comment, and she glanced at his face for the second time. She felt a small sense of horror as she recollected where she had met the man. *Oh my God; this is Mr Kobayashi. I met him at the airport*, she gasped Inwardly.

Shihor raised her eyebrows, surprised that her father seemed to know Alima. She nervously ran her left hand through her long straight hair. The woman Alima presumed to be the mistress of the house also dropped her jaw, in shock to see that these two people seemed to know each other.

The man Alima had recognised paced back and forth in front of her. 'I assume that you have no place to stay and no visa to be in this country, but you rejected my offer of help at the airport, right?'

Alima sensed the look of disapproval on his face, but before he made further comment, she pleaded for help, plunging into a lengthy excuse for what had happened at the airport.

When she finished her narration and plea for forgiveness, the frown on Mr Kobayashi's face said it all—he had not comprehended her plea.

She paused and deliberated with herself about what to do.

She had to change his mind, as she had nowhere else to turn.

Suddenly, she had an idea, though she was sceptical. 'Please wait. I will be back in a minute,' she told Mr Kobayashi.

She rushed into her room, collected her backpack, which she had retrieved earlier from the train station locker, and hurried back to the room. She handed it over to Mr Kobayashi and then finally managed to look up at him through watery blurry eyes. She took a deep breath and whispered, 'Please, I need help.'

Unable to keep the tears from sliding down her cheeks any longer, she retreated into her room and started to pack her bits and pieces into her bag.

The two girls and their father came into the room and asked her to stay; the family would take the risk of accommodating her as an illegal immigrant. They were so kind, caring, knowledgeable, and easy to talk to that all her fears were put to rest. They took an extra day to meet as a family and get to know each other.

Through their meeting, Alima came to learn that the girls' biological mother had passed away during Akemi's birth, and the young mistress of the house was an old friend of Shihor, who'd had a crush on her father. So it came as no surprise to Alima that there seemed to be a turbulent relationship between the girls and their age mate stepmother.

In no time, Alima realised that despite Mr Kobayashi's age, he still took great pride in his appearance, taking more time on his hair than anyone else in the family. He also wore slim-fitting suits and shiny shoes daily, unlike most ordinary Japanese salary men on the Tokyo subway.

Twenty Four

Alima was assigned to the family supermarket. Her first day at work was full of surprises. She realised how rich the Kobayashi family was. They owned a giant supermarket that hosted sellers offering a variety of goods, ranging from food to clothing and amusement boutiques.

She could not hide her joy and surprise at the noise and lights at the game centre. She watched young people take funny pictures and modify them as they wished before they got the printouts in the form of stickers. She was also fascinated by the loud music that played as the guys who worked there shouted constantly at the tops of their voices, welcoming customers or offering them different items and deals.

She was amazed at the efficiency of the waiters and shopkeepers, who were extremely polite and made customers comfortable. They showed much respect for almost everyone and were ever ready to apologize over anything, even if what they were apologizing for was no fault of theirs. What Alima found most striking was their non-stop smiles.

*   *   *

For six months, Alima earned a steady salary, better than she could have imagined, and the joy of it showed in her beauty; she turned heads. Curiously, Shihor started to be surprised at her father's generosity towards her friend, Alima.

Alima was also surprised by the sudden change of the man's attitude towards her. Soon, he told her, 'Stop calling me Dad. Call me Kobash.' The next day, he sent for Alima, asking her to join the family in the hall to watch a world cup football match between Japan and Belgium on the TV.

He then asked her, 'Come and massage my neck. Only your hands look strong enough to relieve the stiffness.'

Alima obeyed, and when she placed a pillow over her lap, he removed it, laying his head directly on her lap. Her heartbeat increased, and she felt uncomfortable as she could feel his head pressing against her womanhood.

He started entering her room late at night to ask her about her day at work without knocking, sometimes finding her in underwear. She had reservations, and she felt inclined to confer with Shihor, but she kept dismissing her concerns, perhaps out of fear she might be ejected.

More disturbing for Alima was that she soon noticed a cold reception from her dearest friend, Shihor, with no apparent reason. Alima, too scared to confront Shihor for any reason, managed to talk to a neighbourhood youngster about her deteriorating relationship with Shihor.

'Please, I am scared to talk about that family,' the young girl told her.

'Scared?' Alima asked.

'Yes, scared,' the girl replied pensively.

'Please tell me, what do you mean?' Alima pleaded.

The girl opened her mouth to talk but paused and drew in her breath. '*Kowai naa*,' she began nervously. 'The Kobayashis are a very powerful family.'

Alima replied with some spirit, 'I thought so.'

'Mr Kobayashi is the leader of a very powerful yakuza gang known as the Kuzuntus. Although he is only five feet tall, his two missing index fingers will tell you how tough he is.

Anyone who crosses him finds him lethal.'

The girl paused and took a deep breath again. 'But,' she went on, 'he has to be a strong leader because there are terrifying rival yakuza gangs who battle over territory, and this, at times, end with deadly gun shots. It is believed that he arranged his first wife's assassination for refusing to take his orders.'

Alima nervously looked behind her to be sure no one was around and stepped closer to the young girl, who hastily continued, 'The Kusuntus courageousness ensures that they have control over a hundred miles square of the main land around Tokyo.

'Their true lives and relationships with other is a thing of constant secrecy. The key player in the gang's protection squad is Shihor, his eldest daughter.'

'Shihor?' asked Alima, astonished.

'Shihor,' the girl confirmed. 'She looks very modest and innocent, but—' The girl paused and looked at Alima sternly. 'Take my word, she is a bruiser,' she added. 'Her main job is to identify potential rival gangs and mark out defence strategies; she is also responsible for keeping a close eye on every member of the gang to ensure that each remains reliable. No matter how relaxed she looks as she goes about her daily routine, she, as well as everyone else in the family, is always in a state of high alert.'

The youngster cautioned Alima not to tell anyone what she had told her. After the two had parted ways, Alima contemplated the danger of living with this extremely kind family.

Thursdays were her normal day off, and almost always no one stayed at home on her days off. She preferred to sleep rather than risk going out. One Thursday, she was home and, she thought, alone. The main entrance to the house was locked, but she left the door to her room unlocked, though closed, assuming it was safe to do that within the house. In order to shield her eyes from the daylight that shone through the light curtains, she pulled her blanket over head, as had become a habit for her.

Barely awake, she thought she could make out the sound of movement somewhere in the house. She held her breath and listened carefully but heard nothing. Soon after she had relaxed again, she heard the same sound. Then she heard what sounded like someone knocking on one of the doors in the house. She was sure the knock was not on her door but, alarmed, she stormed out to check what might be going. Everywhere she looked, it appeared as if she was, indeed, at home alone. Relieved and finally sure she was only hearing things, she walked back to her room and slammed the door behind her.

Standing right in front of her, a topless figure with a raging erection pointing from his boxer shorts appeared. She looked up, and there was Mr Kobayashi staring at her. Alima could smell his breath, which was thick with alcohol. Scared and confused, she looked away and apologized for no apparent reason. She trembled in a sudden rush of fear and retreated towards the door, but he stopped her, motioning her to come nearer to him.

He beckoned her to step back from the window and towards him. She did so without hesitation. He commanded her to get down on all fours. Scared to disobey, she did as she was told, knowing exactly what he was going to do.

She tried to work up the courage to say something and opened her mouth in readiness several times, but was too frightened and only managed a faint audible sound.

Mr Kobayashi leaned towards her with one hand cupped behind his ear and, said 'What did you say?'

She managed another look at the man and, with a huge effort, she spoke in a frightened whisper, 'Condom please.'

He hesitated for a couple of seconds. Then he dipped his hand into the front of his boxer shorts and pulled out a shotgun. Alima's face registered her surprise. He hurriedly placed his index finger against his lips, signalling her to be quiet. She was frozen with fear. Even before he had made a threat, she had been too scared to resist.

She hated what was happening so much that she closed her eyes and cried silently. For about five minutes, the man did not move. Before Alima could realize what was going on, a gunshot rang out, shattering through her window. Mr Kobayashi fired two gunshots back. A loud wailing noise was heard outside her window, and almost immediately, a car screeched away.

Although relieved that the man's actions had saved her life and was not what she had feared, the incident confirmed the stories she had heard about the family.

She was assigned a different room, as hers had previously been Mr Kobayashi's bedroom. He had abandoned it after a similar failed attack on his life some years ago.

Twenty Five

For days, she kept all of her concerns to herself, but the fear that things would get worse persisted, and her only option was to flee.

She made it a point not to be at home alone again. One time, rather than risk staying at home alone, she opted to brave the bitter winter cold and travelled with Akemi to Naeba Ski Resort in Niigata. The resort was regarded as one of the best on Mount Takenoko.

With absolutely no knowledge of skiing, Alima chose the most elegant pink coloured skis and boots to match. She received some professional instruction, which helped her get off to the right start in a short time, and she enjoyed the lesson. Despite some few falls during her preliminary trials, she joined Akemi at the top of the mountain. 'Like with anything, you'll improve the more you do it,' Akemi kept assuring her.

Given that she had never before skied in her life, she was excited when she made a first tentative run and managed to stop without falling over. With this sudden success under her belt, she felt more confident and descended a rather sharp slope. Her speed soon increased, and she started struggling to cope. She stumbled and fell to the ground, tumbling head over heels, and by the time she had recovered, all her confidence had dissipated. Too terrified to stand on her feet, she sat dejectedly in the snow and the light rainfall, which started to increase, making her even more miserable.

Despite wearing layers, including a warm knitted hat and woollen gloves, to protect her body against the constantly changing temperature, her fingers soon became cold and, her nose started running. She decided that she'd had enough; she signalled to Akemi and made her way to the lift back towards the warmth.

Akemi joined her briefly in the lodge. After the two girls shared a beer, Akemi, who was a skiing enthusiast, left to enjoy the reason she had come to the mountain.

'Hello there,' a foreign-looking man in his mid thirties said as he approached her. Then he added something that Alima had never heard before. 'I admire your looks.'

The influence of the beer made her smile back at him. They almost immediately, as if they had no choice, entered into a lengthy conversation.

'My name is Julius. I am a Nigerian,' he told her.

Alima could not hide her joy to meet a fellow African, but sceptical about men from Africa's most populous country, she decided to ask him some personal questions. 'What do you do for a living?' she began.

'I am just one of the many foreigners globetrotting for a better life, and I ended up in a factory in Japan.'

Eager to impress Alima, Julius quickly added to his status.

He explained to Alima that he had since found his way out of the factory, turning a weekend gig selling second-hand clothes at flea markets into a full-time job retailing hip hop apparel. 'Today, I own four retail stores in Tokyo and two in Osaka,' he said.

A little nervous but quite excited, Julius knew that every young Nigerian has inherited an image problem that limits him from highlighting any genuine talent or character he may have. He knew he'd have to address this issue if he wanted to impress this beautiful woman. He reflected upon this as they spoke.

Meanwhile, Alima also found reasons to hope as her new friend spoke frankly about his accomplishments and the issues Nigerians faced when doing business in Japan. He condemned Nigerians who were engaged in unlawful activity but also disapproved the outdated preconceptions in Japan that seemed to effectively render businesses or establishments owned by foreigners, especially black Africans, vulnerable to profiling.

Two days later, Alima decided to steal time to meet her new friend, who soon promised to marry her so that she could get a visa and stay in the country legally. Aware that she was not capable to get a job, an apartment, or sign a legal contract, she knew she should accept his proposal. So she gathered what she would need in order to leave the Kobayashi home.

She took her blanket, two sweatshirts, a jacket, boots, socks, underwear, a hat and gloves, her cell phone and charger, a list of important names and phone numbers in case she needed help, a toothbrush, tampons, and the house keys in case she might want to return some day.

Worried that Mr Kobayashi might not prevent her from joining her new male friend, Alima told Mr Kobayashi one afternoon that she planned to move to Tochigi to live with a relative she had accidentally run into at the Shibuya train station a week ago.

Without hesitation, the kind and generous man said, 'Certainly, you can move anytime you wish, and you are always welcome.'

She was relieved, and the next morning, she was escorted to the train station, where she boarded a train to Tochigi to meet Julius.

Julius, who seemed like a very nice guy, met and welcomed her. He was very outgoing, social, fun, confident, and full of life The young couple went out to the movies then afterwards, the old-fashioned way, they went to the restaurant. That was the very first time Alima had felt intimately connected to someone of the opposite sex. Her first romantic kiss was unforgettable.

*   *   *

Twenty-one days later, Alima and Julius were at the dinner table. Alima looked gloomily at Julius. 'When are we getting married?' she asked.

217

Julius, who was full of smiles and gulping a spoon full of jollof rice into his mouth, paused and frowned at the question. After swallowing what was left in his mouth, he drummed the table with the back of his spoon.

A week later, Julius told Alima, 'I want to marry you, but I have to go to Nigata to divorce my wife before we can marry.'

'Did you say your wife?' Alima asked in shock.

He replied thoughtfully, 'Yes, my wife.'

'But you told me you were single?' she managed.

'Yes, but not exactly.' He paused for a while and scratched his head. 'I really want to divorce and marry you,' he added. 'But I will need about 800,000 yen, and I have only 300,000 for now.'

He looked at Alima again and walked over to her.

Cuddling up against her, he said, 'Please, just give me a few months. I will save up enough to get out of my marriage.'

Alima could no longer hide her disappointment, but desperate not to back down, she made a proposal.

'I—um—I have some savings, which I could lend you,' she told him.

Very glad about the unexpected proposal from the graceful girl, Julius directed a rare smile at her. 'Are you sure?' he asked.

In less than a minute of making the offer, Alima reached for her bag and brought out 500,000 yen.

The next day, Julius, promising to return the next day, boarded a train to Nigata to divorce his wife.

Twenty Six

Julius approached the house at dusk and peeped through the blurry windows. The light was on, but he could not see his wife's image. He waited, rehearsing his story, and when he saw the image of his wife in the house, he marched towards the door. He stretched out his fingers and knocked.

At first, there was no response, but the door opened suddenly. 'Hello!' his wife beamed with excitement upon seeing her husband. She was a chubby, round woman in her twenties with considerable beauty.

Receiving a cold reception from her husband, she cried 'Julius!' her voice rising with emotion, 'what is wrong? Are you all right?'

He made no comment, but blinked several times, forcing tears. He felt a surge of relief when his wife noticed the tears in his eyes and tried to console him.

She became restless. 'Would you like something to drink before you tell me what's troubling you? Have you lost your job or something?'

Finally, he took a deep breath and began, 'I—er—lost my dad.' He burst into uncontrollable sobs.

Julius was crying so hard that his wife could not resist her own tears. 'When did he die?' she asked.

'This afternoon,' he told her, 'at the hospital. He died of a heart attack.' he added.

'When will you go for the funeral?' she asked. 'I can go with you if you wish.'

Julius turned to his wife and replied, 'I wish, but—' He paused and cast his eyes down, nervously pacing the room.

He stopped and said, 'We have to divorce because I have to inherit my father's kingdom right after his funeral in Nigeria.' He added, 'My family will be looking forward to that, so—' He lowered his voice and added, 'I'm sorry. We have to go our separate ways.'

Both Julius and his wife became speechless. His wife took some steps away towards the window.

*I should have married S*huske, she thought, regret surging through her. Barely three years ago, she had been with Shuske, her Japanese boyfriend. The two of them had grown up together in church and shared a very happy life, and he had offered to marry her. Then she'd met this guy. *I refuse Shuske and marry someone I met only six months earlier*, she recalled hopelessly. She quietly pondered what she should do next.

Thoughts clouded her mind but, wanting to suppress her anger, she yelled out, 'I hate you.' She stormed out of the room, slamming the door very hard.

Julius, not wanting to hurt his wife's feelings any more than he had to called out to her softly, 'You just didn't understand me,' he began. He tried to explain how this lack of communication had continued and the marriage had simply drifted further apart. But she didn't seem to understand his explanations, and neither spoke to each other again for the evening.

Though she composed herself after leaving the room, she said nothing to Julius until the next morning. She dressed up and covered her eyes in dark sunglasses and led Julius to the city hall, where they signed and completed the necessary divorce documents.

Julius felt a surge of relief, but he didn't show it, for fear of blowing his cover. He sustained his sober mood and hastily packed his clothes, disposing of anything he no longer wanted whilst his wife watched on, still in shock.

In the end, as he was preparing to move out, his generous wife asked him, 'Do you have enough money?'

'Er—' He hesitated.

'You can have this,' his wife said, handing him 300,000 yen.

Julius's heart lightened further; he was delight to receive the unexpected extra cash. Without shame, he collected the gift, said a final goodbye, and was off.

On his way to the station, he smiled proudly to himself and kicked the air in excitement. 'It was easier than I thought,' he murmured, 'but, er, poor girl.'

Twenty Seven

Alima got her marriage certificate, and she received a temporary alien card two weeks later.

Within a month, she and Julius had succeeded in gathering all the necessary supporting documents, and they posted their marriage application to the immigration centre for visa consideration. Alima learned that that she and Julius may be invited to the immigration service to validate the request before a visa could be issued.

Surprisingly, two months after their marriage, the loving and caring Julius changed into a different person. He slept all day and stayed out all night. Alima wanted to express to Julius how she felt about this, but at the same time, she didn't want to hurt her husband's feeling and risk jeopardizing her chances to get a visa, so she suffered in silence.

As this lack of communication continued, they drifted apart.

On the last day of the third months of their marriage, Alima got a phone call around 7.00 p.m.

'Hello, is this Alima Julius Almond?' asked the voice on the phone.

Her heartbeat increased, 'Yes this is,' she replied.

'I am Koji; I'm calling from the Japan immigration centre in Tokyo. Can I talk to your husband?'

'Yes, please hold on.'

Alima retreated into the bedroom and handed over the phone to Julius. After a brief conversation, Julius confirmed, 'Yes, we will be there on Thursday at 9.00 a.m. Thank you.'

It was the call Alima and Julius had been waiting for. They had just been invited to the immigration centre for an interview for her visa application.

Julius, before leaving to attend to his recent schedule that night, told Alima to ready all necessary documents and passports for tomorrow's big day. Alima was surprised at how glad her husband seemed.

I haven't even known whether he likes me, she said to herself.

He promised to be back in time for their big day and then headed out, leaving his wife in the dark as to his whereabouts.

*   *   *

Alima woke early. She prepared her breakfast, set her husband's portion aside, and modelled her grey dress, which clung to her petite body, in the mirror. Then she waited for Julius.

She thought she heard something outside and paused to listen. Then there was a knock on the door. She raced at the door and flung it opened.

'Alima?'

Her heart started to thump as she was greeted by two policemen. She saw no sign of her husband.

'Yes, I am Alima, she replied sharply.

'Your husband has just had an accident.' The police officer who was doing the talking took a short break and added gently, 'He died on the spot.'

The shock of the news rendered Alima mute. She said nothing but only shook her head, pacing aimlessly in the corridor.

'Do you have anything to say?'

She shook her head dejectedly and, unwilling to look at anyone, slumped on the floor.

Alima, recovering in hospital four days later, awaited deportation. A visa could not be issued without her husband. There, she gathered some information about her late husband.

*   *   *

It was 3.00 a.m., 1 August 1998, in Singapore. Benatu's mind was racing, and she stared at the blackness, wondering,

Why can't I get to sleep?

She had been waiting on death row for nearly three years.

Without any knowledge as to when she would be executed, she always kept her hope alive that one day she would be set free.

Benatu's appeal had been lodged nearly two years after her conviction. Further applications for either reconsideration or judicial review were made but to no avail.

The criminal justice system in Singapore was among the many throughout the world that had a backlog of older cases. A small handful of applications for appeal to review fresh claims of innocence, all of which had taken a very long time to be decided, had successfully found their way before judges. Of these, only a very few fortunate applicants had received positive decisions. And many of the applications were refused outright.

The majority of appeal applicants had been waiting for quite a long time to hear anything, and Benatu was no exception. Like the many applicants still awaiting decisions behind bars, Benatu was oblivious of her appeal's progress. Not even letters were sent to convicts to keep them informed. So she was unaware that her legal team had recently been scrambling to file a motion delaying her execution by the rope.

With the execution looming, Kaolin Phua Chu called the leading judge, Judge Sung Kwao, at 3.00 p.m., asking if they could convene late that night in court to suspend the execution of the girl and enable the court to examine the evidence for her appeal.

Judge Sung replied, 'You lost, time is also lost. But, It's not too late.' With those words, Benatu's last hope of survival has not been extinguished.

Early the next morning, two male guards, both of whom looked strong enough to control Mike Tyson at his prime, pushed into Benatu's cell and took her by the arm. She asked what was going on, but neither man said a word as they led her out.

She had gotten used to such treatment. Each time she had been taken to meet the warden so that she could be considered for clemency by the president at the end of every year, she had been similarly dragged from her cell.

But her excitement turned to worry as they passed the warden's office, heading towards a green door on the left-hand corner far from the warden's office.

The door opened, and she was led through another door.

About forty meters away, there was another door, also painted green. On entering the second room, Benatu observed an anteroom with chairs. It was a large space with a cross hanging high on one wall and a small altar.

'No, no! Please no!' Benatu suddenly refused to walk, and she cried out in terror as the reality of the situation dawned on her.

The guards had no other option than to drag her. She kicked and screamed, calling out her mother's name.

She was led into another room that had been concealed behind a red curtain and onto a high platform. Both her hands and feet were handcuffed, and she was blindfolded.

A few seconds later she was guided back to the altar.

Although she could not see, she sensed that a few crowd was watching from the other side of the glass.

'Do you have something to say before your death?' a voice asked.

The two guards waited for her to respond, but she said nothing.

A moment later, a hood was placed over her head and the noose of a thick rope was slipped over her neck.

As the guards standing by the controls to the trap door beneath her readied to push the button, Benatu made a noise, indicating that she wanted to say something.

The hood was temporarily taken off.

'What do you want to say?' a voice asked.

She took a deep breath and said, 'I am not a criminal. We were only in exile, searching for, a home'